The Girl Who Couldn't Love

I0649591

The Girl Who Couldn't Love

Shinie Antony

SPEAKING
TIGER

SPEAKING TIGER PUBLISHING PVT. LTD
4381/4, Ansari Road, Daryaganj
New Delhi 110002

Published in India by Speaking Tiger in paperback 2017

ISBN: 978-93-86702-30-2
eISBN: 978-93-86702-29-6

10 9 8 7 6 5 4 3 2 1

Typeset in Arno Pro by SÜRYA, New Delhi
Printed at Sanat Printers, Kundli

For Shaji

'If I chance to talk a little wild, forgive me;
I had it from my father.'

—William Shakespeare

Chapter 1

This time before the blackest bird known to man opened its beak I knew who was coming to dinner. He had made his way to me last week on the terrace of a local architect whose parties tend to be a boozy flaunting of renovated properties.

'You live in that white villa by the beach,' he had said.

I gave him a cool look, though taken aback. I took my time responding to this opening line, full of over-familiarity, unsure then as I am unsure now of his intentions. Introduced to me as an artist, at first glance he seemed to live an indolent translucent life made up completely of sequins, the kind I see as sin. If I was tying myself up in knots with my guilt over not doing enough, he made a virtue of his uselessness. 'What do you want with me, I am killingly dull.'

He looked delighted. 'I am insane about dull. You see, I am high drama, I *need* neutral.'

'The self-proclaimed bad boy,' I said, yawn in voice.

He winked. 'The self-proclaimed good girl.'

Giving him a pained look I turned to a widow with readymade sob stories who received me, conversationally speaking, with open arms. I did notice him here and there, an integral part of loud lamp-lit laughing groups, but some gut instinct made me not look, not listen. I had this clock-set life I was proud of and nothing and nobody could alter the tick and the tock of it.

So it came as a surprise when I walked into my home after a hard day at work, teaching insolent adolescents the rudiments of English grammar, to find him ensconced in my drawing room chatting up my semi-blind mother.

They both looked up mid-laugh, mid-anecdote, as if I was the intruder. I feigned a smile.

'Have tea with us,' he said, oblivious to the irony of hosting me in my own house.

'I don't drink tea,' I said, still smiling that strange non-smile.

'She doesn't drink tea, no sweets, won't touch rice…' my mother launched into her usual litany.

'I have already informed him, ma, what a bore I am.'

They laughed again, disproportionately loud, as if I was a hilarious little thing. Adding over my shoulder that there were indeed some beverages I drank without reserve, I excused myself to my room, to wash and change. By the time I came out, he was preparing to leave.

'Roo, you tell him to stay. He may listen to you,' my mother said.

'He must have friends his own age he wants to spend the evening with. How can we monopolize him like that?'

'Roo?' he said, shaking his head as if in wonderment. 'What a lovely name.'

I gave him a discouraging nod, lest he felt free to use it. 'My mother is just too lazy to say the full name.' I didn't tell him this was what my father used to call me, that after his death my mother used it not as a term of endearment but to resurrect him between us when the mood took her. Also, 'Rudrakshi' was one consonant too many; thankfully, one is exempt from mouthing one's own name.

I walked him to the gate, more to see him off the premises. And he knew, if his Pied Piper smile was anything to go by, that I was curious, generally curious, about him. But I was no brawny-tawny rat tumbling after anyone.

He looked at me sideways. 'So what do you do, apart from looking so… attractive?'

'It's a fulltime job,' I came back blandly. 'No time for anything else.' You can't take me out of the shop, I have a bar code.

His cycle was leaning against a hedge ahead—how had I missed it on my way in? He paused, one foot on a pedal.

'Have we met before?' I burst out without thinking, because it occurred to me right then that we may have; that would explain away the mild déjà vu. 'I mean before the terrace thing?' But the moment I asked this I realized how banal it was, this feeling we had met before just because at some basic level everyone looks the same. A nose here, a mouth there, two eyes, limbs four—how different can anyone look from anyone? Same species, he and me.

Again the slanted look. 'We were always walking towards each other, with a dim memory of never having met.'

I tried to look like, yes, yes, I know which famous poet said that. He cut through with an 'I composed it for you, Roo, on the spot', leaving me a little cross.

After he went I studiously avoided asking my mother anything about her impromptu guest, afraid it would come out all censorious as also kick-start an avalanche of unwanted laments from her; of being too lonely, of me not making an effort, of this, of that. I did not want a migraine of my own making, I wanted a quiet evening with my Marquez. And perhaps some wine.

But my mother took it upon herself to enlighten

me about our recent visitor. 'His PhD was on papa's books, you know. He came to tell me that. Such a polite boy.'

I felt a frisson... of some long-forgotten feeling. 'Oh,' I said. I had not looked at papa's books, mostly literary criticism essays on Shakespeare, in a long time.

'You know how papa was, always in his students' lives. Not like you, you keep such a distance from the children you teach. You are not a teacher from here.' She touched her chest to indicate the heart, but her hand was on the right side of her chest.

'I know, ma,' I said on reflex, not wanting a negative catalogue of my teaching methods yet again.

She sighed. 'He took me back to the old days. To when your father was up at the crack of dawn, ransacking his own library, the bookshelves, for the smallest reference he had to make in class that day, to get it right. Such dedication...' She lapsed into silence.

'What is his name?' I asked impatiently.

My mother looked back blankly, as if my face and voice were fading into the ether. For a moment there she must have thought I was asking her husband's name and for a moment there she must have forgotten her husband's name. Then she commented on the saltiness of the daal and we quite forgot the artist man and his chattiness that brought papa flickering back to life briefly between us.

*

He appeared in my school next.

I taught tenth-class kids and they were a boisterous privileged lot—this was an upmarket school, with its 'international' tag, imitation cafeteria and no-uniform clause—who thought me a dried-up sexless twig. I had intercepted enough notes between them touching on the lack of my social life to know this; 'She needs 1 in her moth,' a student had scribbled just the other day to another, 'that'll shut her up'—I did nothing but correct the spelling of 'mouth', which was my job.

The principal called me to her office and introduced me to 'well-known muralist, Mr D. Kumar.'

'Hello, Mr Kumar,' I said. What a generic, forgettable, made-up name.

'Hello, Miss Sen,' he responded with a smile, a smile too conspiratorial, as if he knew I was not going to mention having already met him, as if he'd just tasted chocolate.

To wipe away his you-and-me look, I turned to the principal. 'He read my dad's books as a student.'

Invigorated by this bit of information, the principal

launched into an endorsement of him. 'The kids need someone like him. He will be a tonic for them, shake them out of their everyday routine.'

What? The kids had no routine, and made their contempt of any imposed rules clear every day. Giving them a license to gallop around the school compound pretending to daub at canvases was surely inane? Seems I was wrong. Once a week for roughly an hour, the creative Mr Kumar was to come and set them free from their boring patterns, from discipline, from me. Their imaginations, under staid old me, were apparently atrophying. So here I was, getting 1 in my moth, as prescribed.

I nodded, the skin of my face too tight to yield a smile, even a fake one. He threw me little blithe looks as I led the way to the staffroom where the principal, in a breathless voice, announced him to the faculty.

'Rudrakshi teaches English. She will coordinate the classes with you. We are so happy you chose us for this project. You will find the school has an ultra modern approach to the arts.' The principal beamed, a glowing self-congratulatory smile. 'And now I will leave you in Miss Sen's capable hands. She will help with whatever you need.'

Sensing his gloating, I murmured an impersonal assent.

'Can I have your phone number?' he asked amidst the resulting hubbub, flashing what he must think a heartwarming smile.

And how to refuse such a reasonable request? I gave it to him inaudibly like a state secret at gunpoint—he had to make me repeat each digit twice—and then put my phone on silent and tucked it deep into my handbag where its vibrations would be muffled.

I went back home and dived into my books, old, trusted ones with dog-eared pages that I had read before and would read again. Feet up on a cushion, I replace all of real life with what I imagine.

Chapter 2

It was inevitable that this day would come, when he'd be expected home for dinner. The crow cawed and I almost nodded; yes, a guest was coming, whether I had invited him or not, whether I wanted him here or not. Well, this is life, it goes on, new people with new names enter it and all of a sudden the future feels infantile, crawling on fours in all directions without a care.

He was diligent, I must give him that, had done his homework. At dinner that night he managed to thaw me out a little with his relentless good humour, with his absolute refusal to take offence. And mother, mirth papering over the cracks on her face, reminding me of herself from a distant past when she used to appear in my school with packed lunches on the days all was right with her world. It was reassuring to witness again this side of her, the side that knew what was going on, read headlines of the day, and reacted to hot water on skin by saying 'ooofff'. She turned her partially unseeing eyes on him, Kumar, and regaled him with laughs as he did her with story after story. References to papa came into most of the reminiscences and it was like he sat at the table with us. I know this because mother's reaction to the food was ditto his that night; 'the curd should still be milk, setting only as you spoon it up' and 'salad so crunchy it bites the teeth'.

Born in an urban nook of Bengal, married off to the most eligible English-speaking bachelor her parents could lay their hands on, she had photograph albums aplenty in her possession of those early days. Engagement, wedding, honeymoon, holidays. Posing permanently in black and white or lurid touched-up colour against tree trunks and buffet tables in trousseau best, carrying her anxiously happy eyes from one frame to the next. She had come to Mangalore a pampered bride, a brightly plumed migratory bird, and at rare times like these, when a stranger was drawing her out, with pink cheeks and shining eyes she stole back to her newly wedded days as if to a tourist spot.

Chandeliers glinted off, she told Kumar, her husband from day one. His face, even in his photographs, had the radiance of a rising sun, didn't it? So obvious how celestially blessed he was.

That all this white light pointed to divine racism never bothered ma, who thought nothing of reducing gods to electricians. I sat back and let it all wash over me, in some way giving in finally to this onslaught by an outsider, his unforeseen entry into what was a clockwork robotic timetabled existence comprising of morning alarm, school, goodnight. Of ma's background bickering and the maid's paltry pilfering. I floated free of myself, sedated by the wine brought by him (wait a minute, how did he know what wine I liked?), and watched like a disembodied spirit from the ceiling this cosy domestic scene. We looked like a trio of old and good friends, kin almost, catching up on story so far, waiting with pleasure for the rest of the story to unfold. Cute, a cliché, like cut-outs. An ad for a soft drink.

'Do you know the students find you awesome,' I told him, lilting the 'awesome' like the kids did.

He laughed. 'Everything is awesome to them.'

At the gate he thanked me and I thanked him, the night all peaches and cream. How did our faces get so close, noses almost touching, I don't know, but suddenly there we were, contemplating, I think, kissing. I would like to say I withdrew first, for what was there in physical intimacy but the possibility of novelty and the surety of future humdrum? I made a peculiar keening sound and he rubbed my back as if it was colic. We did not say bye;

I think we both knew this was an interrupted moment, a present continuous moment, a moment that lay in wait somewhere down the clock.

*

I met him once a week in school and at least twice a week at home; he was a different type of fixture in my life, a moving, bobbing one, like a balloon in a kid's hand. Unlike the potted plants and morning assemblies, he was a mobile flexible musical oil-paint-smelling presence; his impermanence in my life, not to mention sudden advent, lent him an amiably 'catch me if you can' air.

Blobs and splotches, I messed up large white surfaces with them. Blindfolded, I threw paints like knives. Kumar tilted his head and whistled each time, like at masterpieces hung in a gallery. And his comments, that I affected not to hear, had me return to my work when no one was about. He showed me palettes, brush sizes, how a secret undercover dab catapults a colour to another level. The mute submission of clashing shades when mixed, why letting go frees up a fast colour to be another colour, a slower one, a softer one, a sighing one. Smaller colours hidden under larger colours, pigmented and speckled. Coming out gun in hand around an unexpected corner: 'The name is Bond, James Bond.' With fingertips a glorious never-before tint, I smudged everything with my new Midas touch.

Mother was right, I did consciously maintain a distance from the students, but she wasn't right about why. It was not that they would contaminate me, it was more the fear of me contaminating them. They had this lack of awareness, this cross-eyed running into anything anywhere, as if roses came thornless, as if life owed them a jolly good time just because they had been brought forth unasked; why look down on that trust? Their furious multi-colours brought me face to face not with their sunny dispositions as I had presumed, but their inner world of tumult and late-night angst, as if they knew, exactly as I did, that it was best to chirp now because nests were lined with nothing but straw.

'Sir, sir, sir!' They milled around Kumar, looking and acting their age, not like the weary jet-lagged travellers who came to my class with their one-liners and overnight cases, sure I'd harm them if they didn't harm me first. There was the flap of their invisible wings in the air on Tuesdays, the day allotted to Kumar to come enthral.

Kumar.

The mundane in me replaced now by a feverish waiting, I was, in the end, any other woman, who waited puberty onwards for a Prince Charming, for a member of the opposite sex to carry her away to a land far, far away. Though what I told myself was that the basics of art were far more interesting than I thought, hmmm.

Sporadic texting between us began; he the initiator, me the reluctant replier. What you reading? That's all he asked. And I would text him the title of the book in my hand. I am a superfast-express reader who will read anything anywhere anytime, my compulsive need to read placing quantity way above quality. And maybe I wanted to show off to him, so that every time we could talk about different books, from Rilke to Richmal Crompton to Rick Riordan, from hymns to haiku, from the biography of a saint to a mountaineer's memoir. The quotes I sent him were always profound, the profundity too over the top to be personal. This was non-intrusive, I convinced myself, this was…academic. And if his texts smelt of linseed oil, it was a nasal defect on my part.

The infinite allure of unknown men! Ask any woman, that's what takes them down in the end.

*

Staffroom banter left a lot to be desired. Resembling a jungle at nightfall: cheep-cheep grr meow, survival and territorial sounds and occasionally a smaller animal being dragged off by its neck. Invisible earmuffs protected me against the vitriol. The voice in my head so clear, so sharp most days that others and their concerns settled into a background score. Occasionally some teacher would point at me, or smile, and I had to turn down the volume of my thoughts and hear about their diets, their in-laws, their overgrown backyard grass, their EMIs.

Male teachers were few; a PT sir and now a drawing sir. The rest women in various stages of menstrual flow. 'Got my P's today,' they'd announce. P's were either on, had just ended or just begun, as if it was a race, conversations milling round cramps, stains and champion absorbent pads.

The other thing that united them was The Fringe. They had what they called 'bangs' over their foreheads; a frill of hair that fell into their eyes, obscuring vision. This, they said, reversed age. What ma, who had attended one annual day function in the school and saw all of them in a row, called the Sadhana Cut. One of them even cut and trimmed bangs for free in the staffroom itself, so that teachers could leave younger than they came in. A tasselled head was a life skill. My decision to comb back my hair or have a side parting was met with a sigh.

This makes you look younger, that makes you look thinner... If you were on their right side, the teachers fussed over you indefinitely. They had tried this with the principal when she was new, cooing over the jasmines in her hair at some initial meeting, how fresh they looked, how sweet they smelled, mmmm. She carefully took the flowers out, saying anyone could have them, they were plastic.

From the first day the principal had taken to looking at me fixedly during meetings, as if addressing only me. This not only meant I had to look awake but was seen as crown prince, so to speak. A misunderstanding further exacerbated by my being as unmarried as she and presumably as workaholic. To them I am principal in running. Which keeps them inwardly hostile but outwardly kow-towing.

The principal, petrified of social media and what she thought the general permissiveness of the current lot as opposed to my indifference to all of that, often bracketed us together as 'people of our generation' though a good deal older than me. The teachers, secretly believing us to be men, waited for us to die of prostate cancer.

Most of them dawdled, unable to wind down intensities with the last bell, mouths still moving even as spit ran dry, jaws set to survive nuclear holocausts. I was always packed and ready, my feet facing the door, much before that ring. I flew out of there like I had just finished planting bombs.

*

Frowning at the prospect of correcting test papers, I walked home and into my room without looking up. So the shock of seeing him that day was all the greater.

He was sitting at my desk. In my room.

I could literally not say a thing. What was he doing here? I gave him a composed look, all my earlier suspicions about him springing back to ferocious life. *Why was he here? What did he want? Who was he? No, really, who?*

'I heard a loud noise,' he said.

'From this room?'

'Not sure. I thought Aunty had fallen or something.'

'Her room is that one,' I said, pointing out of the door, to the opposite end of the corridor. It was not that his statement was not believable—it was possible to dash into a place without having been there before, with an altruistic look on your face—but the way he spoke of the chances of ma having met with an accident was a bit too casual. Because here he was, sitting at my desk, unruffled. Surely if he thought she had hurt herself, he would be charging from one room to the other, searching for her till he found her safe and sound.

My gaze steady on him, I only shrugged. 'She usually naps at this time.'

'The front door was open, so I walked in. And then I heard that loud noise…'

Open? I had unlocked it just now with my key; the maid left roughly an hour before I reached home, during which time my mother usually slept or watched TV. If the TV was not switched on, like now, it meant the former.

'The maid must have forgotten to shut the door behind her,' I said to diffuse the slight tension in the air. Was he poor? Had he come to rob money from us? Even well-off people stole for sport, I'd heard. I must check if all the gold and cash were still here after he left, what little we had of it anyway.

'Tired?' he asked, tenderly. Feigning tenderness. I ignored the dip in his voice, like I do in all male voices.

'Not really. But I am going to be. I have a lot of papers to correct.'

'Then I won't keep you. Off I go,' he said cheerfully, making for the door.

'Wait…'

He turned around, a little-boy grin on his face, an eyebrow up. But what could I say? I shook my head, as if I had forgotten what I wanted to say. 'N… nothing. Bye.'

After he left I sat on my bed for a while. Something did not make sense. What was the purpose of coming here so early in the day? He had never done this before, he'd always come early or late evenings until now. Okay, no point being rattled too long. I got up, checked on ma and my purses and jewellery, very meagre and disappointing to any self-respecting robber. I found everything intact. Less or more as I remembered.

During dinner I said not a word to ma, who in turn said not a word to me. Doubtless she thought I was sulking and sulked right back at me. On such nights, with silences crusting over, no one put out the plastic garbage pail and no one put the milk coupon in the little jute bag by the gate.

It was only when I was back in my room to sleep and pulled out a fresh pair of pajamas from the drawer that I saw the cupboard in disarray in places. My antennas were up; he *had* gone through my things. Maybe I had returned too early, maybe he had thought he had all the time in the world to loot us and I had foiled his plan to plunder. Or did I in my morning haste to locate a matching dupatta get all careless with the ironed clothes in my cupboard?

Me or him, it was one of us.

Chapter 3

Christmas holidays were looming large. My aunt—ma's sister—arrived from Pune. This was the norm. On school vacations, she would come to take over household matters, leaving me free to roam. Not that I wandered far and wide, pledging all my vacant hours to an old friend's business. She ran a boutique store called EeeDee (the initials of her name—Ela Dhar) on the outskirts of Ooty, and that was where I set off to when I had the time. Armed with the latest books in fiction, non-fiction and poetry, I arrived at Eeedee's place—that was what everyone called her these days—by lunchtime. I liked the fuss-free atmosphere at her house. She was single by choice like me, which meant a lot of fluff talk, like why aren't you married, when will you settle down, who will look after you when you are old etc, was automatically off the agenda.

'What do you fear most in someone trying to get close to you?'

'Bad breath,' Eeedee said very seriously. 'I mean, thank you for your interest but let's brush, okay? Nothing wrong with a little toothpaste. Best invention, if you ask me. Imagine in ancient times, all those kings and queens in silk and pearls holding their noses as they bowed to each other.' I rolled my eyes with an empathic ha-ha, going back uneasily to that moment by the gate when Kumar's lips brushed by mine. Oral hygiene had not been on our minds then.

'Back stories,' I told her, having given it a lot of thought on the bus-ride here. 'The parts of a person you will never know. What they left behind.'

'Hey, lay off Greek tragedy.' She wagged a finger. 'Makes you mistrustful. On with life. Have you brought me any old books of yours?'

'Old?' I laughed, taking out all the glossy new books I had brought her. She sat up squealing in the middle of the bed, the books open and tumbling around her, her hair little-girl tousled, eyes no longer sleepy. She held an open page to her face and inhaled deeply. 'Books, they never have bad breath.'

We were two peas in a pod, a library-shaped pod, where we read book after book after book, and lived happily ever after in the happily ever afters. Which man on earth, however Orlando Bloomish, could compete with a bestseller or a classic or even a nursery rhyme? That's my real nightmare, that I will run out of books to read one day. To this end, I hoard reading material. My house has in its most hidden corners books I am yet to read, books that will jump out at me from behind a sofa screaming, 'Surprise!' when I am old and bookless one day.

I have known Eeedee from childhood, from the time we were schoolgirls in pigtails, her hair frizzier than mine and pigtailed more messily most of the time, and this much we had in common: putting fictional characters before real ones any day. While other girls in our school frantically worried over what to wear, we frantically worried over what to read. In our dreams we ran in slow motion towards storybook men.

Someone called up Eeedee then. I could make out from her end of the conversation—'I hardly know him, sorry' and 'how can I tell you if he is good husband material? I mean, I never married him'—that it was a routine matrimonial check by some matriarch enquiring about a suitable boy for her darling, quite possibly useless, daughter, to be divorced as soon as she was married off. Compare this with the last call Eeedee got at night, where she went on and on, quite forgetting her guest—me—about a movie based on a book, and which was better, the movie or the book.

I let her words wash over me, this clever critique of a book I too had read and felt the same way about, thinking with some amount of pride, 'I gave this girl her first book', and dozing off to her memorized paragraphs from it, which felt exactly like waking up to birdsong for other people.

*

The next day I went with her to her boutique. I did this when I was with her, hung around with her in shop or home all day. The dresses this season were more Western and Eeedee happily discussed embroidery patterns with me. When she was on the phone—did she *never* leave that phone alone?—I noticed a young girl peeping into the shop.

'Come in,' I said. 'Come in,' I said again when she made no move to enter the shop. I went to the open doorway with chimes hanging over it and invited her in.

She came in hesitantly, not meeting my eye and just stood there.

'Yes?' I said after a while. Then, as if waking from a reverie, the girl walked towards a dress. And there she stood, till Eeedee made a face at me, still talking on the phone.

'Can I help you?' I asked in a hushed way, like I had heard Eeedee do with people who came into the shop.

She started and then shook her head, her hand still on the dress. I looked at the dress. It was a soft fabric (mal, I learnt later) with a large flowery design (kalamkari, I learnt later) and had a drape look to it (anarkali, I learnt later).

'Would you like to try it on?'

She looked at me then, as if the idea of trying it on had just occurred to her too.

'Can I?' she asked and I thought her voice trembled.

'Of course.' I took the dress off its pretty stained-glass hanger and handed it to her.

She actually ran to the trial room. She was in there for a long time. Eeedee motioned with her eyes.

I knocked on the trial room door. 'I can help, tell you if it fits…'

She said nothing in response to this but the door opened a little, then she tiptoed out. You got the sense that her heart was a mad thing in her chest. A fish in a net, a felon mid-heist.

Soothingly, I first commented on the dress. It fit her perfectly and she looked transformed whether by the dress or the joy of wearing it at last I cannot say. 'Looks good on you,' I said.

A quick up-down of eyelashes. 'I know,' she said simply, stating a fact.

'Would you like to buy it?'

This was when she went back to her rabbit look. She retreated into the trial room, changed back into her own clothes and without a word fled the shop. It was like she'd never been.

'What just happened?' I asked Eeedee.

'Oh, this girl. Such a change from shoplifters. You know I have had women come in here and putting on dresses and kurtas under what they are wearing, such well-off-looking women, and that's it, they walk away scot-free, without paying a paisa. Recently...'

'What were you going to say about her?'

'Her? She's a sad case, that one. Comes in often, looks at this same dress, touches it and leaves. Doesn't have the money, I guess.'

That night before I slept I thought of the marooned look on the girl's face when I asked if she'd like to buy it. Were all of us in the thrall of something we could not afford?

*

The two weeks of my holiday consisted of cups and cups of hot chocolate sipped in Eeedee's large balcony—the house belonged to a bachelor uncle, who had bequeathed it to her when he had to be put away in a nursing home for being irreversibly old, only so, she said, she could carry on the legacy of no breeding. She was in turn going to will it to the adopted kid of a friend of hers.

Eeedee was no cook, so we ate jam sandwiches and two-minute noodles most of the time. Once in a while she took me to a café nearby where we ate more heartily. She was also a great believer in silences and letting things be, so there was no compulsion to chat, gossip or update her on anything. She did ask about my mother cursorily and I answered without going into the rancour and complicated anger that attended most of our—mother's and mine—interactions. I was peacenik for now.

The balcony sat like a cosy nest on a tall branch. Too many leafy trees fanned out high above us, forming a green sky under the blue one, a second sky.

Eeedee lived well within her means. Sexually frugal, rusk at mealtimes, water for wine. Even her medical conditions seemed on a shoestring. The murmuring heart, an unset fracture, single kidney, ovarian cyst, juvenile diabetes… nothing too serious. Body something to be walked, incidental. No mirror, mirror on the wall.

She put down the book she was reading and cracked her knuckles. 'This new mythology trend puts too many obscure men and women centre-stage. Kubja, Putana… the sidekicks going yak-yak-yak about themselves on the pretext of talking about Krishna. There's a reason they were voiceless in the first place.'

'But protagonists can be a bit of a bore,' I disagreed, stretching myself, 'self-obsessed as they are with developing their own character, exit lines and conflict resolutions. You know, delusions of grandeur, all "I thought", "I said", "I did". It is the wino or wet nurse who tells it like it is because they are no one. Always watch out for the tongueless. What they are not saying.'

She put up a hand. 'Miss, Miss, I know what I want to be. A magic bean in Jack's back pocket. Or the goodies in Red Riding Hood's basket.'

I lay back on the recliner, dreamy. 'And me the glass slipper silly Cinderella so carelessly left behind.'

'I've always wondered, Roo, how that did not turn to rat or rubble at the stroke of twelve. Just think about it. Everything else did.'

'All alone, pining for my pair, my mate! And a hundred yuk feet, misshapen, bunioned, swollen, smelly, sweaty, forcing themselves on me!'

Eeedee dozed off to my martyrdom.

*

The girl was back. I had two more days before leaving and was helping out at the shop and here she was with the same lost look in her eyes. Again I beckoned her in, again I cajoled her into trying out the dress, and again she rushed out hurriedly without a word.

I was puzzled. I looked at the price tag of the dress. Rs 3,500.

'No wonder!' I exclaimed to Eeedee. 'This is expensive for most people. Can't you price it down for her?'

'No can do. Even if I want to make nothing from it, it doesn't make sense to do this. What if she is back for another dress? You know me, I am not a Shylock type, though I wish I was, would make life simpler for me! My own margin is hardly the barrier, it is the price for the appliqué work, for the tailor… I am sorry.'

On my last day the girl was back, and this time I spied a damp eye. 'Can I buy it for you?' I asked impulsively.

She gave that gasping look she reserved for me when I attempted to engage her in conversation.

'I have a niece your age,' I lied on the spot, so as to lessen her embarrassment at receiving a gift from a total stranger. 'And you remind me of her.'

'And does she also have a man who dumps her when she is pregnant?'

I was left speechless. My imaginary niece was a hundred percent chaste. And if biologically possible, would impregnate men herself.

'I cannot wear this in a month or two. But if he is back…' She shrugged a slender shoulder.

I got it then. The dress was to be a celebration. The dress was to coincide with his return, and then her life would be perfect. Ah, us idiots, we are the same the world over.

I could no longer help her and was glad the mystery was solved, just in the nick of time, before I left. But that night after the light was switched off I still saw her face, with that half-hopeful, half-shuttered look. I thought of her lying in her own bed somewhere, dry-eyed, hand curled on lower belly, still disbelieving of a child, and hoping against hope that she was reading his silence all wrong.

Chapter 4

Back home I was on auto-pilot for a while, straightening things up; the fridge was empty, the groceries had run out, the ceiling fans were grimy, mother's annual medical check-up was due and the organdie cushion covers up for a hand-wash. In between all the dashing about I learnt that Kumar had been a regular visitor in my absence. I stiffened a little but made no comment. It was pointless warning mother of anything; she would simply blab to him, her craving for company overriding common sense.

When he came by one evening I realized I had been holding my breath. I was, despite myself, happy to see him. Is it possible to gleam and gently sway like hair in a shampoo commercial just because someone walks into a room? And he seemed happy too, as if I was exactly who he walked into rooms to see. For some reason that girl's face came to me and I wanted to tell him about her. But when I did it came out all wrong.

After dinner ma chose to retire early, saying to Kumar, 'God bless you.' I was nonplussed—where does she pick up this trite stuff?

With ma gone and the TV on, he and I chatted about current affairs, the newsreader's hairstyle and the typos in the ticker (the last was down to me). I made some tea and he drank it dutifully.

'So where were you? Aunty said you had gone to meet a friend.'

I nodded.

'A guy?'

I made a face. 'I'm not young any more.'

'One is never too old to make friends, surely.'

'It's not youth,' I said at last, 'but stars in eyes that drive one to others. Me, I have a stye in each eye.'

'Oh no! Someone broke your heart.' He leaned forward, eyes dancing in faux sympathy. 'Tell me all about it.'

I refused to make light of it or to divulge any details. But I did say, 'Women everywhere are waiting for the call. Which will never come. Men play with them on good days. On bad days they are with other women.'

'Ouch.' He looked at me more pointedly. 'So who did this to you?'

'No one,' I said with gritted teeth. 'And now I must sleep.'

'Alone,' he said, more matter-of-fact than mocking but it got to me.

'Yes, alone alone alone! Why, would you like to sleep with poor old me just so I am not alone?'

'Yes,' he said.

*

I woke up with a headache but with the piety of someone who had averted further disaster. I had bid him goodbye after that quiet 'yes' of his that had rung in the air like a gunshot, got rid of him before I changed my mind and did something I would regret forever. The last thing I wanted to do was haunt little shops trying out this dress or that to make me look desirable to the one man who would never look at me again.

'Thinking of your tea,' he texted sometime during the day.

'Better than drinking it,' I shot back. I can fry water. Keep it on the gas burner and forget all about it, it's a gift. My culinary attempts look like stool samples. And when the smoke alarm goes off I never connect it to the kitchen, examining every cranny in every room till the pan itself is completely cooked.

So that was that. Pass made. Pass dusted off. Now we can all go back to whatever it was we had been doing. If the camaraderie was going to be a bit off from then on, so be it. It happens to all women sooner or later, some man takes advantage of proximity to explore probabilities and permutations. Why must awkwardness be the realm of only women?

*

In school the next day he drew up a chair next to me in the staffroom during a lull.

'I have something to say. Please take this the wrong way.'

I laughed a little at that and waited.

'The day you caught me in your room, I had just gotten curious. You are such a…'

'Such a?'

'A suspense.' He raked back his hair with a wrist-watched hand. 'Your eyes say "keep out". I guess I just wanted to see, to begin with, what your room looked like.'

'What do you want me to say to that?'

'That you want to see my room too.'

I laughed again, more unreservedly this time. 'You are a strange man and I am not sure you mean what you say.'

'Say what you mean then.'

I raised the middle finger of my left hand in an 'up-yours', cupped it with a palm and brought it to him like sheltering a lit flame. 'Ah,' he said contemplatively, 'the size of your metaphorical penis.' And as he left, casually over his shoulder, 'Are you on WhatsApp?'

I shook my head without regret.

'How do your lovers communicate with you?'

'With their eyes.'

After that we were on an equal footing, not too close, not too distant, with only an expectation to be mildly entertained by the other. Each time we met and talked it was a different meeting, a different conversation. Sometimes we ignored each other, sometimes we greeted each other like long-lost friends. He'd ask about my mother and other teachers would chime in, knowing him to be a family friend. Someone would ask me for his phone number or when he was coming to class; he was the life and soul of the staffroom, the one for whom the fringes flew. The two of us were seen as friends, and if anyone was curious as to how I, a pissed-off-looking spinster at least a hundred years old, could garner such a lively young pal, no one actually came out and asked.

Between him and me was that quick, furtive look now and then that stayed on my skin like a rash. And the occasional text that made no sense.

All right.
All right what?
Does it matter?
No.

Pings with no text. A blank space. Silence. To which I text back my own wordlessness, my waiting, my watch-this-space. And once in the middle of the night his: *Now.* To which I could only demur: *Later.*

*

The local architect guy had made another palatial house, this time two hours away from here. The invite was only to a select few, and an overnight one; we were to admire the edifice an entire night. I accepted, after the help agreed to sleep at home so that mother was not alone that night. Glittering blindingly on the inside, I made my way to the housewarming. This time when he walked up to me I did not look away, in fact, could not look away, our eyes stapled together. Two throats cleared, ahem and ahem.

'Your room is next to mine,' he informed.

'What does that mean?'

'My room is next to yours.'

'All rooms are next to someone's, aren't they?' Was I forestalling, was I flirting—I didn't know, but there was that sufficient lack of reserve between us now. He sat on the arm of my chair sipping mocktails (a teetotaller!), and though we never spoke directly to each other, our toes kept colliding, my right leg crossed over my left, his left over his right. Eyes meeting and re-meeting in mock apology, we didn't for a moment stop playing footsie. When, while turning to someone behind him, my breast brushed his arm, we froze for a second, a set of idols. No oxygen up either nose.

There was some bad singing. When it was his turn and Kumar gamely agreed to sing, I kept my eyes averted from him through the song, which was in my mother tongue, Bengali. He had told ma that his first tongue was English, which had puzzled poor ma. 'But what is your *real* language, what you spoke at home growing up?' she asked many times.

He sang as if speaking, in a low monologue, a popular RD Burman ditty about unattainable girls, over far too quickly for me to take it personally.

'Mone pore Ruby Roy
kobitay tomake ek din koto kore dekechi
Aaj hai, Ruby Roy, deke bolo amake
tomake kothay jano dekhecchi.'

When fingers pointed at me, I coughed in picturesquely tubercular fashion, but no go. I was forced to ham a childhood rhyme that I sensed Kumar listened to intently, especially the ending, which made everyone laugh but him.

'So I kissed her little sister
And forgot my Clementine.'

I elbowed him. 'What's with the long face? Am I so bad a singer?'

'Reminded me of a Malayalam hymn written by a German missionary. Volbrecht Nagel. Same tune. *Samayamam rathathil njan…*' he hummed that bit. 'In the chariot of time. Played at funerals.'

'How morbid!' I pretended to pat down goosebumps on my arms. So was he from Kerala or was he a translator of songs or, more likely, a fellow-Googler?

In the middle of some gory murder story, recounted by a young pouty journalist on crime beat with fake ringlets and an equally fake air of vibrancy, sure to spur gorier stories until early a.m., I picked up some fruit from the dining table and retired for bed. He texted immediately, 'What you reading?'

'No book today, alas. Eating grapes.'

'Slowly?'

'Medium speed.'

In the Bollywood-themed loo, where Meena Kumari kept a tragic eye on proceedings from the wallpaper, I brushed my teeth, grinning. I knew I would sleep well that night. Usually, at home, there was always the chance of mother calling out to me—mostly for what she couldn't remember by the time I reached. Here I somehow felt safe, in this house filled with a raucous rowdy gang of assorted ages and, yes, him next door. I was running in slow motion towards him… I must have nodded off when the sound of a text message woke me up. I rolled over and picked up the phone sleepily, sure it was him with a good-morning smiley. It was from Eeedee.

'That girl who used to come to touch the dress? Killed herself.'

*

Breakfast was a subdued affair, a part of me elsewhere. Could I have prevented that death? Had she told me the truth? Maybe she was a theatre artiste, fooling people at the drop of a hat. Through it all I kept thinking: I should have bought her that dress. Should have insisted on buying it for her. My ruse hadn't worked, that was why she refused. It smacked of charity, of some sort of superiority on my part. The niece story hadn't been good enough.

Kumar noticed my preoccupation and had refilled my coffee thrice before I realized what he was up to and stopped draining my cup. 'Look what you made me do!' I was going to pee non-stop all the way back!

It was a Sunday and though I half-hoped Kumar and I would be paired off in the same car home, it did not happen that way. I was stuck with the Sarna twins. Who were by and large okay except for a voice an octave too high. To be stuck for over a hundred minutes with that level of shrillness—the twins had a habit of repeating each other—was trying, and it was touch and go whether one would make it back with eardrums intact.

He texted me immediately. *Your hair.* Making me touch my hair self-consciously the whole drive back, wishing it longer, thicker, blacker, straighter, softer…

I seized up when the twins mentioned Kumar right then, like my head was glass and they could see inside. 'Who is he to you?' one of them asked. Before I could reply, the other said, 'Who is he to you? Cousin?'

Good moral people who wanted me to hang out only with male relatives. So touching, I almost nodded. 'No, not a cousin. We are not related.'

'So much like you,' said one twin.

'So much, much like you,' said the other.

'We can drop you off first and then go home. We don't mind, we have each other for company,' they had offered. An offer I waved away with some brilliant acting, and I can hear them even now, murmuring in piercing decibels, 'She is so alone.' And the murmur back, 'So, so alone.'

After they got down at their home, I was grateful for the fifteen minutes of silence till I reached mine. Also vaguely depressed that the age gap meant no one thought about us *that* way. The illicit excites only by its constant threat of exposure.

My phone beeped then. It was him being him, saying only, 'How?'

'What?' I texted and sat back, listening, hand curled around the phone. One could get addicted to imaginary conversations.

I had a dream that night. I was wearing that dress, the dress the dead girl had wanted. And she said to me accusingly in a stage-whisper, 'You took my dress.' I woke up drenched in sweat; it had felt like a visitation. I kicked off the sheets and, of course, the AC cooled me down quick. Later I could remember the dream, but not what she looked like. Either she had looked like me or I had looked like her, for the one thing I do remember is we were Siamese in my dream, like two versions of the same person. Damn those Sarna twins!

A word about my dreams. Some walk me down roads as vehicles whiz past, little zigzags of light, metal and mirrors, and there I'd be laughing an evil laugh as trucks ram through me. On a pier balanced delicately, arms out, a stumble toppling me into water, where I turn into a seal or sardine and swim away like we are wont to in dreams.

I once even saw a woman made of vaginas walk the street and men stopping to board her like a bus. But these are everyday everybody dreams, dreams to recall when small talk is made. It is the other one I never mention. When I dream of… nothing, not a thing. Just this great gaping hole of a dream. Sleep after sleep, dream after dream the same empty. An empty full of such emptiness! During the day I dry-sob just remembering. In the night I wake up, tears pouring down my cheeks.

It lies in wait in places I least expect, this nothing where a dream should be.

Chapter 5

I woke up briskly, maintaining an air of getting things done, barking orders at myself, impressing myself and others with my tongue-clicking impatience, making all the pending phone calls and calculating bills to be paid, but feeling more and more like a bubble-wrapped wrong delivery in a long-distance truck.

Come over, he texted sometime during the day, as if he could see me, clucking about, headless chicken.

'Small print can't handle.'

'No small print.'

'How can you calmly plot sex?'

Not, he said, calmly.

I was less jittery the next day. Perhaps my hormones were settling down after too many circus shows. He of the boyish smile, how harmful can he be? I closed my eyes in a pseudo-Zen way. I wish him well, don't I? I wish him someone with long, black, thick, shiny, soft, sun-dried hair…

Being on top of my form still left me back-footed when he texted, 'You are right.'

'About?'

'Right for me I mean, you.'

And the hormones were up again, hanging from pegs in a hurricane.

*

It was seldom that we had an 'us' moment in the staffroom, given that he came in only once a week and buzzing as it was on most days with staff and students and ma'am this and ma'am that. But when the school organized a day trip in April first week to kick-start two months of school holidays, we both signed on pronto.

Oh, I knew I was getting all knock-kneed and pigeon-toed for nothing, that he would come out whistling at the other end and me with more of these words I can never tell anyone, so that by the time we were in the bus sitting together, thighs pressed inconspicuously against each other's, some level of sobriety had happened, thank God. I almost got away with it too, this new touch of frost, but maybe I wanted my bluff to be called, my double-talk to be exposed. After refraining from joining in his breezy small talk with the others and letting my gaze fall off his a fraction of an instant before our eyes met, I waited.

It wasn't too long, as my woman's instinct had predicted, before he joined me at the edge of a manicured lawn. 'What happened?' he asked in such a quiet reasonable voice, I almost grabbed him to me then and there.

'What?' I asked.

'This whole distance thing you are doing, like you hardly know me.'

'I can't…' I struggled for words. 'I cannot… It is not you. I feel I drive away those I most want to keep. So best to do it before, you know, not after.'

Gazing into the distance, hands in the pockets of his jeans, he shrugged. 'What do you want me to say? You are trying to take your future, our future, into your own hands. I cannot promise, I cannot foresee. We may last a weekend, we may last a lifetime, who can say? But how can unknowables hold such sway over what we do know?'

'What *do* we know?'

His eyes found mine. Briefly. Like the first two stones rubbed to make fire.

'And my age?' The crow in my Aesop's fable had dropped enough pebbles into the pitcher, raising anxiety levels to the brim. 'I am older than you.'

'I have no respect for chronology.'

I watched him walk away, all youth and conceit, seemingly leaving it to me, the pursuit. So I am to stand still and do nothing. To breathe in and out, to not think, not feel. To keep feet right where they are, hands by my side and not worry about which word to say and what move to make to keep those who say they love me keep on loving me.

On the return trip the students were boisterous, singing and laughing. We sat far apart this time; him in the front, me in the back. We were careful not to look at each other while casually commenting on whatever the others were saying, in an attempt to appear normal, sociable, but mostly lost in our own thoughts. But when the bus braked rashly with a deafening grinding noise we immediately looked at each other, and only after he saw that I was okay and I saw that he was okay did we rush to the students in the aisle who had lurched over mid-song.

*

'What you reading?'

For the first time I dared to ask, to make the first move. This had taken me an eternal internal debate, but it was the first day of May and I had all the time to be daft.

He texted back immediately. *You.*

I knew what he meant; he had borrowed a book I was teaching, inscribed with my illegible notes. 'You shouldn't say such things to me,' I typed and deleted. I sent a more honest: 'I feel I am usurping your desire under false pretences. I'm no sexpot.'

Your insecurity leaves me free to ravage you.

I could say nothing more. I felt hoisted on the needle-point top of a slope, but I also felt immensely foolish. In the mirror I could see the crow's feet on my face from where I sat; if I were served on a table, men would go on a fast. So many young women twiddling their ass out there…

Another text. *Thinking of me?*

His message was a set of lazy letters lying back indolently in the tiny square light of my phone screen. Yes, I replied, and stared at my sent message, disbelieving.

I think of you all the time.

I made a face. Yeah, right. But sent a safe '?'.

Undressing.

My breath hitched down a hairpin bend. Then I jabbed at my phone. 'Lights on or off?'

On, he said. *On my desk.*

'Sounds like office to me,' I tried to wrest control back, infuse levity. I wanted to go back to the bookish distant professorial type I imagined I used to be. Also, he only wanted to shock me because of my advanced age and lack of looks, so I was going to be unshockable. 'Today's Labour Day. It would be fitting.'

Long and slow.

'Good night,' I said primly.

Muah.

And though his muah went to my head like some strong nose-watering throat-burning monosyllabic hooch, I switched off the table lamp and scrolled up previous texts with imbecilic zeal.

Then came his *What you wearing*?

This was the time to take a fist to his phone-face; this was what bored men world over asked bored women. But I said meekly, 'Pajamas.'

Drawstring or elastic?

'I feel I'm talking to a tailor.'

No, you don't.

My only weapon, self-mockery, was failing to come to my aid when he asked, *And under that?*

'Barbed wire.' Then I switched off the phone.

I was practising amnesia, trying to bleep out what I knew about men. First phase: have arms, will hold. Every phase after that: have arms, will withhold. Baby-talk was a prosthetic tongue men could detach any time they wanted. The bass note in 'take it all off' is missing in 'where did you keep my glasses?'

Chapter 6

That morning in June I opened my cupboard and had nearly turned away when I thought I noticed something amiss. I looked again; the shelves looked neatly arranged. Too neatly. Must be my mother or maid and their annual itch to springclean. I would never find a thing in here! The road to tidy wardrobes is paved with good intentions. Still, I made the customary check. Dug my hand deep into the back and rummaged wildly in the left corner. It was missing! The diary! Yes, it was!

I couldn't scrabble around for the diary all day, I had to leave for school. Today the new academic calendar began and all teachers had to look alive on the first day of school. I was uneasy the whole day and my mind kept going to the logical culprit—Kumar. But why? Why not, asked an inner voice. He wants to know what you think of him, he wants to know if you think of him at all. Thank

God I was not an itsy-bitsy girlie-wirlie little thing to scribble down my *feelings*.

I couldn't wait for school to end. I hurried home and searched frantically all over again. And there it was. Had it been there all the while? Had I missed it in my haste to find it the last time I looked? In my panic? I began to breathe easy, but I could have sworn it hadn't been there in the morning.

'Did anyone come home?' I asked my mother casually.

She looked taken aback by the query. 'Why?' she asked nervously. 'Why do you ask this? Has something happened? Wh… who is coming?'

I assured her that nothing had happened, no one was coming. I pretended not to see her facial tic or the blurriness of her actions, the tumbler crashing in the kitchen and her fumbling her way to bed. I had long ago run out of ways to calm her.

I called Eeedee. The call was long overdue.

After pleasantries, I asked, 'And how did that happen?'

'What?'

'You know, that girl dying.'

'Oh that. Happened ages back. I just got to know now. I saw a picture of hers in the paper, under the deceased column. It said 40th day ceremony. With her name, Erica something or the other. I would have thought Harpreet. My…'

'And when did you see that?'

'The day I texted you, obviously.'

I went back to the text message, which I had not deleted thankfully, and checked the date. I counted forty days back. She, the girl who came to touch a dress, had committed suicide on the day I left Ooty, the day after I met her last.

'Who were you speaking to?' ma asked, coming out of her room, her voice a tremor.

'No one,' I said. I took the diary out and opened it at random.

He is here. In the house. I cannot speak. I cannot write. If he sees me, he will snatch you, dear diary, and keep you with him. He will shred you to pieces and throw you into fire. He will pull out your tongue. He will pull out my tongue…

I read no more. That same lack of air hit me. I was back in my childhood. With an effort I walked out of the room, taking deep breaths.

'What's that?' came Kumar's voice.

'What?' Was he stalking me? How was he already present in the house when I had heard no doorbell, no opening of the door?

'In your hand.'

I looked at my hand. I was still holding the diary. Quickly, I held it behind me.

'A diary!' he said, clapping his hands in glee, manufactured or real I couldn't tell. 'You write a diary!'

'This is a child's diary.' My voice was curt.

He put a hand to his chin, pretending he had all the time in the world. 'What kind of a child were you?'

I turned around smartly, leaving him standing there asking his stupid questions, and kept the diary carefully back in my cupboard. For a moment there, the past had looked like the present.

*

That evening my chatter was not up to the mark, and he kept slipping me questioning glances now and then, but I couldn't, I just couldn't, get my act together. His face when he asked me 'What's that?' had been so much like … papa's.

'How much have you read my father?' I asked him during a gap in the conversation.

My mother peered at me. Perhaps she minded my tone. 'I was his student in a way, as I read all the four books over and over again, so as well as any student knows his mentor, I would say.'

'Which play of Shakespeare's did his first book go on about?'

'*The Tempest,*' piped up my mother before he could say anything.

'Is that right?' I prodded him. 'Is that right?'

'Why are you so…upset?'

'Who in this play, Kumar? Tell me.'

'Miranda. I mean, it was Prospero, but his musings on Miranda.'

At any given time papa went on about any play by Shakespeare. It depended on his mood. It depended on the day. He was a whimsical man, going from tantrum to nobility at a moment's notice. I was brought back by Kumar saying, 'He loved the father bit, I guess, seeing as he was himself a father. That is the book he dedicated to you, wasn't it?' I nodded. 'He was Prospero, I could see that. Which would make you what, Miranda?'

I laughed. Mother peered at me again. She did not trust my laughs. Not any more. I once laughed so hard I needed medical attention. It does not look good for a daughter to laugh when her father is laid out dead in the drawing room. Hysteria, said everyone. No, mother liked my laughs to be laughed less. She would like me never to laugh at all.

'I am biddable, you are saying, in awe of her Superman father in a cape.'

'I didn't say that,' he said even as mother made some sibilant noise, as if to douse the lit wick in me.

'Maybe you got him all wrong, you know, maybe he is King Lear, so let's not forget Cordelia. The daughter accused of not loving enough.'

He nodded gamely, with a disinterested smile, like his mind was on bigger things, important happenings outside this room. 'So who are you? Miranda or Cordelia?'

To him, the pair of them womanly women, identical twins. When it comes to women, a carbon paper is inserted between all male brains. Lacy hair, baby-butt skin and double D cups. I could just say 'either or both' and he'd move on to another topic. Every girl a daddy's girl, men want to hear that. They are all dads to be, transporters of sperm. On call in case the world was ending.

'Hmmm,' I pretended to consider. 'Both loyal to their father, but in their own ways. One a student of her father forever, hanging on to his every word, perennial schoolgirl. Ms Lear, however, almost Mr Lear in how practical she is, how she won't get misty-eyed about the word love. Not what you'd call an amorist.'

Kumar never took his eyes off me. 'Both perfect daughters though.'

Daughters anyone would die to sire, daughters who came through. But what about the girls themselves? How did they cope with their control-freak dads who knew what was best for them at all times? 'Yes, perfect daughters, nothing wrong with them, it was the daddying that messed them up,' I said.

Mother got up, gripping the armrest of the sofa she had been sitting on. 'It is late,' she told Kumar with uncharacteristic emphasis and the usual unfocused look from her failing eyes. 'You must be sleepy.'

He jumped up to leave and ma hurriedly mumbled, 'God bless you.'

I laughed again, that slightly out of control laugh that riled ma up. I looked at him soberly then, letting all my loneliness show in my eyes, and said only one word. 'Stay.'

Mother, despite her bad sight, gave me a disapproving look. That 'stay' reeked of feminine wiles. That 'stay' was supposed to disable any sound judgement on his part. And he stayed.

'You win,' he said, looking more like the victor between us. We heard mother shut her door behind her with a bang. He grazed my cheek gently with his knuckles. Was he trembling? Was I?

'You are beautiful,' he said, infusing the words with such raw pain, as if truth was a tooth pulled out of his mouth.

He had no idea how much thought went into the dim, soft lighting at my home. Under harsh illuminating sunlight I am another story. 'What do we have in common?'

'Stunning looks?'

'My dad. You are his fan, I am his child. The thing is, he has other fans, right? You are one among many.'

'But only one child.' His voice flat, face in profile.

'Only one child. One,' I echoed, looking intensely at him, willing him to return my gaze.

When he did we sat there looking at each other for the longest time. Wary of lingering on each other up until now, downright terrorized to tell the truth, our eyes couldn't stop once they started. Unblinking, unsmiling. Like he was entering me oh so slowly.

An urgent incoherent embrace ensued. We became … real. Shadows who found their way back to their bodies. Sleeping with other people had been play-acting, silhouettes mating. Techniques flew out of my head, what I had done before, what I did well, how I appeared right now, was desire distorting my face—for the first time I did not worry, I did not tie myself up in knots frantically planning ahead my next move. I just was.

Took him by hand to my room where we consummated, sans any frills, whatever misalliance had sprung up from the great nowhere within us the moment he asked me if I lived in a white villa by the beach. This was the villa, the villa by the beach. And this was the bed in that villa by the beach. The villa was white, my sheets whiter. I plucked away his hand on my mouth and tuned out his shhs—I was going to be loud, make all the noise I wanted to make. My mother's ears, unlike her eyes, were in perfect working order, more functional than average to make up for her ineffective eyes, but this was me breaking loose and my silence was going to be the first to skip town.

I learnt his dainty asymmetry. His two right ears, two bottom lips. A pair but opposable. And the mouth of premonitions, exactly where I want before I want.

He tucked my hair back, put his forehead to mine, like there was no rush, infinity was us. 'At last in you.'

'I will die,' I told him.

'Of?'

'You.'

Chapter 7

Sometime during the night my new lover had left me, my bed and my house, in that order. He had tiptoed out into the dark, leaving me all alone and fast asleep. I woke up, my body aching in all its deepest chambers, and ran to the cupboard. I collapsed against its door weakly when I saw that yes, the diary was still there.

Okay, I told myself the next day at school where I spent a lot of quality time staring into space, so this was going to happen, him and me, only never forget what you know about men: they want to be the only man, but approach women in droves.

A fact amplified by the husband of one of the teachers who barged into the staffroom right about then asking where-where-where was his wife. He dashed about blindly, a small man in a small room, saying only 'where', till he located her bag hanging on her usual chair. He riffled in it, pulled out her phone, scrolled through the messages, seemed to find exactly what he was looking for with an unholy 'aha', and began to accuse her loudly of having an affair. 'I have proof,' he kept saying, waving the phone at us.

His wife, interrupted mid-class, came in with stock denials and a fringe grown sticky with sweat, adding to the fracas. Someone tipped off the principal, who asked them both to leave at once, this very minute, as the students, attracted by the hullabaloo, had begun to flock to the staffroom. The adulteress was suspended for a month for setting an immoral example and all us other teachers, feeling enormously moral, talked about this for hours.

'Doll,' Kumar texted sometime during the day, and I remembered him with an intestinal spasm, my undercover lover.

'Doll has dark circles.'

'Why?'

'You.'

A little while later came a prosaic: 'Birth control?'

I only bled in dribbles and drops now, menopause all set to hit me in a day or two. 'All good,' I replied absently. Later in the day, suddenly insecure, I texted, 'You are coming today, yes or no?' My phone rang. 'Yes,' he said, and disconnected.

In the evening, a flurry of texts led up to his actual arrival; just before he left his home, he asked, 'Starting out now. Need something?'

'Yes,' I texted back, 'A bigger mouth.'

We texted each other furiously, audaciously, bawdy as can be, sitting to ma's left and right even as she went on and on to him about her other ailments, junior to the very senior eye problem.

Mother accepted this new turn in our relationship with more grace than expected. She would sit with us, appearing to be only a little out of step, without the joie de vivre she had previously displayed, without the previous possessiveness, slowly surrendering her guest to me and me to her guest, but nonetheless lapsing into long reminiscences of dad, building him up to the hero he was in her head. Kumar played along, though I suspected him of politeness than real fandom.

In the privacy of my room though our masks came off, or maybe they came on. The floor, the bed, the bedside table, the door... our amorgasm tested all hinges. The one and a half decades or so that separated us in age did not seem to matter in the there and then. His tongue tender at my most vulnerable spot had me reach for him in blind panic, begging him to stop, to never stop, calling out 'please, please, please' over and over again, as I lay there both open and broken.

He engendered in me a vast bottomless greed. For him, for life, for what remained of my youth. To him, I am sure, I was a crude charcoal sketch of two long grabbing hands, with a wide open insatiable maw.

*

Let's make hate tonight. Take off our clothes, climb into bed and pretend we are other people. New faces, new bodies, new love words from new mouths. The names we call out not each other's. The sigh, the moan, the sun, the moon—not yours, not mine. Only the creak of the bed real.

Such caricatures we make of ourselves when the sex is new. All flamboyant antics and showy spending. Eating in overpriced places that serve minuscule portions and getting each other eccentric gifts like enamelled owls and bejewelled bats. In a hurry to create a history, a shared past, to fast-forward to that fond look we can throw the other and say, 'Remember how you… when you…?' not really knowing the shortcut to there.

We began to quote Gibran to each other, and Keats. But when he texted 'The Incident', a poem by Norman MacCaig, in its entirety, we took a break (he called it, rather sentimentally, 'our first fight'—it wasn't but I didn't want to fight with him over that). It was the word 'love' in it that threw me: and not just love but '*fiery with love*', like love forgot to turn off the gas. I wanted no declarations. Not in verse. Not in jest.

'I am a fuck buddy,' I told him. 'I can't make your finger break into a bloody blossom. The sooner you know this the better.'

He seemed to choose his words with care, as if translating a foreign language. 'I strongly like you. The sooner you know this the better.'

Did strong *like* mean weak *love*? Best not ask. 'It is all semantics. You say,' I raised my voice, 'like. I say,' I lowered my voice, 'like.'

'That's just pitch,' he laughed. And since he has an attractive laugh I allowed it to be the last word.

'Am I your type?' This after he had advanced and I had advanced right back, and we were bedridden with lust. Dying from it.

'Who is not my type?' I countered airily. 'Except a paedophile. And that because I'm not *his* type.'

In a preamble to another verbal skirmish in another context, he demanded during foreplay that I say it, say love, say it to him. 'I love you,' I acquiesced, making it clear it was only a bit of nonsense, a verbal snack thrown at a hungry ear.

Later he asked, 'Was it hard saying it?'

'I don't remember.'

'Don't *remember*?'

Time for a newsflash. 'These are lies. Lies men tell women to get them into bed. Lies women tell the men they cheat.'

'Have you ever said it to a man before?' he demanded to know.

'Many men.' Then because it felt safe and expected, 'To my dad.'

With flared nostrils and folded hands and looking for the first time like he truly hated my family, he declared, 'I am not your father.'

And I had nothing to add to this statement except think furiously, 'Even my father wasn't my father.'

*

I am not adopted, in case that is what all this sounds like. I was born in the second year of my parents' marriage and I have no reason to doubt my mother's fidelity. She couldn't get pregnant again, it was biologically impossible, which apparently irked my paternal grandmother into writing my inheritance off to a grandson, but this made no dent in my life, never having evaluated her net worth then or now. I grew up well-fed, all puppy fat and sailor frocks in baby photos, thermometer in mouth every time my temperature shot up even one degree. Whenever I performed badly on stage for school annual days my parents were always there in the front row with matching expressions of pride. I was a mediocre student, chronic backbencher, never making it to the top ten in class but never staying back a year in the same class either. An ayah was by my side always except for the time she had chicken pox. A happy childhood then, if not a happy child. Which is more than what many offspring are accorded by those who make them.

But then melancholic dispositions are nobody's fault. It is just there, inborn, this desire to not meet life halfway, to stand there with hands folded on chest and ask, 'what next?' in a monotone, tapping a foot.

Meanwhile, my new lover planned an out-of-town rendezvous. I went along, not least because I knew the end was upon us. Nothing lasts, no two people find each other exciting eternally. At some point his jokes will fall flat and my introvert ways will begin to pall. I will become 'too silent' and he will be an out-of-work clown. That is just the way it is with men and women. The razzle and the dazzle and then the empty pockets, with no more unending silk ribbons to pull out. And really, one part of me waited almost eagerly for that moment, that first dying of the ardent light in his eye, the first curling away of his fingers from mine. When it would no longer thrill us that we had said the same word together or that I was without underwear beneath my elaborate kimono. Even in the deepest throes of passion a part of me was mentally preparing to be cast aside. No question mark would mar the lines of my face when that happened. *I won't be at your door one day, saying, want me again.*

'Have you been here before?' he asked me.

'Here' was a brutally luxurious hotel showing off all its five or six stars with great opulence.

I shook my head. 'My pay is not UGC scale.'

There were freshly cut roses everywhere and brocade on walls. Wine sparkled photogenically in crystal glasses and cutlery glimmered discreetly amidst piped piano music from concealed speakers. No staff member, reception desk onwards, winked at our unlikely pairing, the obvious age difference and the even more obvious carnal nature of our relationship. Indeed they seemed intent upon making us more randy if possible. The room they gave us overdosed on red. Scarlet, crimson, vermilion, cerise, cherry... Even the shower looked flammable.

'My name should've been Ruby Roy as you sang that day,' I joked. 'Ruby to go with the interiors.'

He picked up an apple, also very red, from the elaborate fruit basket and ate it in two bites, like he didn't want to keep it waiting. 'But we all know it is Miranda—or is it Cordelia?'

'Neither,' I said coldly. 'I am a woman, any woman. It is a survival of the species thing, sudden lusts.'

'You know, I have to admit,' he said, sitting on the bed and taking off his socks, 'a lot of my attraction for you is to do with whose daughter you are. I have admired your father for so long…'

'He was a brilliant professor. He had a way with words. He knew what words can do, can get you. Especially if you are not privy to the power of words yourself. Then it becomes like a superpower he has.'

He paused to look at me, a sock in one hand. 'I wasn't a bad student, if that is what you are suggesting.'

'We make heroes out of ordinary people when we are in need of a hero, not the other way round.'

'Nothing wrong with that, surely?'

'Nothing,' I agreed, but I was laughing at him, at his childish need to get himself a king in his bedtime story about a kingdom with a beautiful princess. The dragon to be slain, the king without a son, the princess who wouldn't laugh, waiting to be rescued—wait, who is the main protagonist in this story? I smacked my forehead; of course it is the pauper son-in-law whom the king pays to make his daughter laugh, or to fuck his daughter mindless to be more twenty-first century, so she wouldn't die un-orgasmed, the poor, poor girl. Modern kings would know their porn or at least some pop-feminism.

'*I'm sure my love's more ponderous than my tongue*,' I quoted Shakespeare, and Kumar gave me a strange look as well he might; those were filial words, not amorous, Cordelia's down to earth aside on Lear, her dad. To make up for my slip, I quickly quoted Miranda's more flowery line to her boyfriend, Ferdinand, '*I am your wife, if you will marry me. If not, I'll die your maid.*' I went down on my knees and hugged his legs, making a joke of not just my slavery but the word 'wife'.

He walked away, leaving me there on the floor, intent on putting his things away in the ornate closets with filigreed doors.

'Hey, I thought men found doormats hot!' I protested.

He came at me, combative. 'I like you sulky. In a bad mood. Spoiling for a fuck.'

'Rooooo,' he cried out later that night, steeped in me, and I held him tight. I could forgive him that much, this shortening of my name I hated with all my being.

Is there any pleasure equal to that of lying naked on your lover right after sex, floppy body to floppy body, sated, nuzzling, demanding nothing but fuzzy warmth? The blind leading the blind.

The weekend went by in a haze. We rarely left the bed. This was our domain, where we lost our all-thumbs clumsiness and came together in pre-choreographed touch, intent only on eliciting an 'ah', an 'oh'. Where my cynicism and his horseplay travelled in the same direction, like two stones pelted at a mad barking dog. Listening only to a voice that said: Now.

And there were moments we exchanged selves, when he seemed lost in some inner dusk and I laughed freely and spoke without subtexts. Were we becoming legendary lovers, I mocked myself, like those tragedy-prone yin-yang twosomes who died locked in each other's arms? But that would be the perfect revenge on my idiot students, who never listened to me in class— their kids having to learn of the two famous lovers who died, well, legendarily. And if we wrote buckets of bad poetry to each other, all the better.

Kumar's raised eyebrow made me giggle, but I refrained from divulging my silly daydreams to him. I merely revelled in the silly. Silly had arrived late in my life. But arrive it had.

Him calling what he saw and heard without me 'such a waste of time, our time'. Him singing Rabindra sangeet: '*Amaro porano jaha chay...*' And when I teased him about learning *my* language, breaking into Tamil lyrics. From a Sivaji Ganesan lullaby: *Kannil mani poley, maniyil nizhal poley*. Like a pupil in an eye, like a shadow in a pupil. So did he know Tamil, I quizzed, or did he just know this one line. What language *did* he speak? Where was he born and where was he brought up? Where was this man of mine made?

'Your turn.'

I shook my head, shy and unused to shyness.

'Not even a *nuna paatu*?' he said.

'What's that?'

'A false song. A song full of false notes.'

His songs, his readings, his declarations of love, his small talk, his ramblings, his disjointed murmurs, his pillow talk, his sweet nothings, his one-word phone calls, his voice, all he had to say, every word of it... I could spend a lifetime listening to him. *Make your sentences long, convoluted, dense but just go on and on, never stop.* I had suffered from silence for so long, I know that now. All those words directed at me, solely at me, made my borders come alive, and within these borders I was a land inhabited again. Birds sang, rivers flowed, boughs flowered etc. Finally, all my fullstops were conjunctions—soft, buttery buts and ands and ifs. All my line breaks now ellipses. Life a book of commas.

Not that life had been unbearable. On the contrary it had been madly hectic with its mundane chores and queries, its bills to pay and clothes to collect from the dhobi, with the father it took away and the mother it left behind. The stand-up and sit-down and keep-walking. But this. This was deep breath on a mountaintop. Mint lining the lungs. Gave me the chance to relive my own life, like this was how I'd be if I wasn't who I was. No longer made up of self-loathing and uncertainty, no more the person who once slept with a man she just met on the table in his office only so she could hate herself some more, I was now this brand new me air-dropped into the middle of his sentence.

'Your nipples are...' his voice trailed off, his fingers like paintbrushes. He had this habit of reaching around from behind and covering them with his palms and asking gruffly 'guess who?' as if they were my eyes.

'Awesome?' I giggled into my wine. He often ran out of words to describe them. Inarticulate in the face of areola, ordinary areola puckered like old bark.

'Very talented. Remember that slumber party when I sat on the arm of your chair and you turned to talk to someone?'

Of course, I remembered. A part of me was still a sculpture back there.

'They said hi to me then.'

'Actually, they need sweaters of their own. Jumping up at the slightest drop in temperature. I used to wear two bras to school.'

He gave me his heavy-lidded sideways look. 'Sometimes I taste milk.'

Uterus in flip-flop I took a moment to scoff, 'You will lactate before me!' I dipped a finger into my glass. 'Here, try this.'

He held my finger to his nose, inhaled deeply and licked it clean. 'Merlot,' I informed him unsteadily. 'The little blackbird.'

He sat up a little, mumbling diffidently, 'That reminds me… I have written a poem. Would you like to hear it?'

I nodded deadpan, hoping he wouldn't embarrass himself and me with something third-rate about the moon and rain. He was young, after all, when such vocabulary felt original.

'It is called *Dive into me*,' he said.

Don't look like a teacher, don't look like a teacher, I begged of me.

He sipped some water, activating his Adam's apple, and began to recite in a solemn voice:

'*I a pool on a clear day*
In the middle of me, clad in me
Feel the tide against
Your naked heart
Gather me in palms
Hold me to your face
And pour me slow
So my tongues run all over you.'

Heart! There it was, the word that demarcated his hopes from mine. 'Here's to free verse,' I said, clinking glasses, knowing his face would fall when I left it at that. We always know if someone thinks our creativity drivel.

After the poem, we spoke little. We drank something, we ate something, we watched something on cable. He turned to me, muting the TV. 'You are my fate.'

'Seal me,' I said in a cheesy way, slinging one leg over his lap. Some men just make you feel so... boneless. Like a satin ribbon flapping in the wind.

'Run your tongues all over me,' I quoted back raunchily.

*

Before leaving I bowed reverentially to the room. 'Thank you for making me see red.'

'You are mad,' he laughed, pulling me to him.

But back in the car during our drive home we resumed our original identities. When we saw two dogs at it I exhorted him to drive right through them. He didn't.

By the time I slept that night, snug in my own single bed, I had tossed out the branded lipstick I bought from the hotel store. First smashed it with a rolling pin till the outer tube lay in smithereens in the manner of broken eggshells, wiped clean the meat-red waxy mess that oozed on to the kitchen counter, bade farewell to former pout.

It had been bothering me, this out of character buy. Something about this man made me not me. When I was with him it was like meeting myself for the first time.

Chapter 8

We made two more such weekend trips, but the magic of that first trip could never be recaptured. Instead there were awkward moments aplenty, like when he bought me a red lipstick in memory of the late one and I could only gawk, never apply, relying on good old petroleum jelly once more. Out came my reading glasses and Kindle. My taste in lingerie began to slip and there I was in very comfy sports bras and granny pants. I could have worn these to the coffee shop below and no one would have batted an eyelid, so wide and long were they. My cleavage was no longer indecent exposure, but an accidental spill quickly covered up.

Nothing compares to that first time, does it? When the flesh quivers and strains like a blade of grass in the breeze, saying touch me, touch me first or I will uproot myself and touch you. Skin slowly bared, joyously, deliciously, little by little, inch by inch, till both are naked, too naked, very naked, naked down to their shadow, so naked that one seems to wear the other. Like crude bombs in backpacks that blow up in crowded marketplaces, the nuts and bolts of our bodies strewn on a bed.

He wants to take you in all the ways there are and you want what he wants, *yes-yes-yes*. Then what? What?

Our conversations turned pedestrian. From his earlier frantic 'don't bathe, come sweaty' right before our trysts, it was a prosaic 'five p.m. okay for you?' or 'so sleepy, can't see straight' these days. Dirty talk on a loop, every last bit a repeat, what we had said before, heard before. As for the new ones, I had a job not giggling sometimes. I imagined him thinking them up in a cold-blooded solitary way, all those hardcore improper suggestions, and working them into conversations in that offhand way. I remember the time Eeedee and I had picked up some desi porn during our adolescence, and the misspelt words that had us incontinent with laughter. 'He took his pennies out of his jokeys,' she would say to me even now, to indicate someone's affair. And I would reply, 'Then they began to moo together.'

Sex, the brightly packed FMCG, best use till ten days of opening. Love had shrunk to L and kisses to xoxo in texts, like our fingers were the first to tire. He still called me 'my love' but more to point out how wrong I was about something than because he was addressing his love. 'My love,' he'd drawl when I suggest detours, untried cuisine, cinema show. It meant no.

On the other hand, paradoxically enough, after the L word, I was afraid he was slowly and steadily making his way to the M word. Men do that, take it a notch higher if declaration of love goes unmet by fluttering of lashes.

Marriage. Not a bad word, not a bad institution, means well, heart in the right place and all that. Even the priests and pundits who by-heart all the vows and mantras to marry people off are devoid of malice, merely doing their job, making a living. I still get my share of matrimonial enquiries. Blame my biceps. Makes old men think I can handle bedpans.

When he cleared his throat I looked up warily. I had to refuse, for both of us. The woman he marries… Some days I did nothing but think of this woman. 'My parents,' he said apropos nothing, 'had this long lovely marriage.' He had told me earlier how they had died in a road accident *together*, italics his. Personally I thought given a choice they may not have valued dying together over living longer *alone*, italics mine. Of course in the face of such unbridled sentimentality at first I only nodded silently. Best to allow people their little myths.

But when he persisted, one unguarded moment

unravelled all my tact. 'Everyone says this. That they come from perfectly content unions. It is, I suppose, our compulsive need to believe that our parents had long lovely marriages. We want to overlook their petty fights and in some cases sleeping around. I mean, just because they are our parents doesn't mean they are idols in a puja room. They are human first, then a dad or mom. And they have bodily needs. Mothers don't sprout wings at childbirth. Nor do their genitals evaporate.'

'But look at your mother. She never remarried though she lost your dad at what age... thirty-five?'

'Hmmm.'

'She is devoted to your dad.'

I nibbled his ear.

'Come on, I am right, right?'

'Right, right? What kind of English is that?' I laughed. By now I was nibbling his earlobe like I was a refugee from a famine-struck area and the feast was dripping down his head. To his credit he recognized a determined erotic overture when he saw one, especially while being gnawed at with such rat-like efficiency.

At night I flossed my teeth. They deserved a treat. For getting me out of an unwanted confession. It had been on the tip of my tongue. To say, 'She is devoted to the memory of a man who died long before his death.' Because it is possible to freeze your faith, keep it in an era of your choice, leash it to a picket fence. If I could shuffle evenings like cards, I would put right on top the one when my dad told me the first story of my life, with that transformed face of his, in a baritone that raises the fine hair on the nape of my neck to this day, with his hands waving in the air, about… It doesn't matter about what, it was only a bit of fiction in the end. But fiction that put me to sleep in a cosy lap of softest cotton, my parents murmuring to each other late into the night, long after I slept, their voices merging with the rustle of butterfly wings in my dreams. Gauze. That's what I briefly became.

*

'I cannot go on like this.'

I looked him over. 'Like what?'

'Without conditions.'

'And what are the conditions?'

'That we be absolutely and continually frank with each other.'

I heaved a sigh of relief. I knew he was trying to pick a fight, but I couldn't have borne the 'let's get married' stream of consciousness I thought I saw coming. 'I am,' I said more earnestly than I would have liked. 'I tell you everything.'

'You must be joking. I tell you a lot. A lot. But the more I talk, the more silent you go. You are so…secretive. It is like you throw up these walls around you. You turn into a bloody wooden bench if you think you are about to—God forbid—actually say something. You clam up. All. The. Time. About the real things, I mean.'

'Next time I will turn into a wrought-iron sofa set,' I quipped.

'There is a man?' he asked tersely. 'A married man?'

My laugh came out inappropriate. 'There is always a married man,' I said with an arch look. I crooked a finger at him, 'Come here, Mr Kinky Pants.' He sat there glumly and I was too exhausted to get up and go to him, to cajole him out of his bratty mood, like a little geisha girl paid to do her cabaret around a celibate sage, or am I mixing up seduction techniques here? I turned over and the next thing I knew I was fast asleep.

When I woke up it was late and he was sitting in darkness, not having switched on a single light, and from his grim profile I knew he was still smarting.

'Take it as a compliment. A woman goes to sleep so soundly only in the company of someone she can really relax with.'

'Or someone she considers non-existent.'

'Oh okay, I give up,' I said. 'Which married man do you want to hear about? The one who couldn't get it up or the one who didn't take off his clothes, not once?'

He shook his head to both—not this man, not that man.

'Tell me then what do you want me to talk about?'

'Let's see. How about your fifth birthday?'

Was that an uncannily picked date or was I too damn suspicious for my own good?

On my fifth birthday I had sat under my bed, frightened out of my wits, as papa went around the house looking for me… *Roo, Roo*, he kept calling. Any minute now he would find me… and…

And nothing.

I laughed an artificial sounding laugh. 'What do five-year-olds do on their birthdays? I cut a cake, opened a gift, and what else? Oh yes, everyone sang happy birthday to me.' I began to sing, 'Happy birthday to you, happy birthday to…' My voice cracked, I could not go on.

'Why,' he said, each word spaced out, 'do I get the feeling you are not telling me what really happened?'

'Because I am not.' I looked into the distance. There was still no light in the room and the lack of illumination, the multiplying invisibilities around me, braved me to say, 'It was the saddest day of my life until then. But you knew that, didn't you? Didn't you?' *When did the Sarna twins take up residence in my throat?* What happened to my normal voice?

'Don't get paranoid, baby. How would I know that?'

At some point during our so-called courtship we had decided mutually to call each other 'baby'. This gave the whole thing an 'it' vibe, or so I thought in my terribly dated way.

'Because somehow you do.' Sotto voce but he heard me. If I expected him to rush to his own defence I was wrong. He merely turned his head away.

'It is not hard to know you have secrets. And that they are roughly the same size as you. You are literally bent with the weight of them. All I am saying is,' he came up behind me and held me in his arms, rocking me gently, 'you have to start somewhere, this business of believing.'

'I am an open person…'

'Yes. But you don't trust easy, do you? Open people can sometimes be the most reticent.'

He was right of course. One can be verbally loathsomely forthcoming in a gushing manner but still not say a thing of import, keep to oneself the most sacred.

'I am an open person,' I repeated, more to say something. 'I opened my home to you, my arms, my legs…'

He exploded. 'This is what I mean. This is exactly what I mean. You say these unexpectedly crude things, fun things, you do them too, but you keep the real you out of sight.'

'Maybe,' I suggested in a small voice. 'Maybe there is no real me. You might be wrong about that. This is all there is to me.'

He shook his head thoughtfully, chin in hand, his long artist fingers distracting me as always. 'Perhaps you prefer under-love to over-love. In the hierarchy of want, you get to occupy the superior spot. Give less, have more. I get you.' A decisive nod. 'Yes, I get you.'

I shoved knuckles into my mouth. Swallowing conciliatory words, words that passed back like bile and vomit into my system. A passing interest wasn't a lifelong oath. He had his growing up to do, I had my remaining life to get over with. Suicidal to think yourself, of all things, *understood*.

I began with proverbs I'd seen hung crookedly on walls, 'No one is perfect…'

He stood up jerkily. 'I can't take this any more.'

I said nothing, just watched him retreat; it wasn't him walking away, it was me receding to the back of some unreachable beyond. Last wavelet in a vast sea. Sick I felt and superstitious. A solo magpie did fly past the window that morning.

*

So that did not end well. We packed our meagre belongings—toothbrush, nightclothes, paperbacks—

and I took a cab, not wanting to share the intimate space of his small car. Not with him glowering and me simmering. I did not, most of all, want a showdown. Who knows what he would end up saying and who knows what I would end up saying? Best to part this way, in low decibels, with a polite handshake. I go my way, you go yours.

I was back in my white villa by the beach. Back on my single bed in my tastefully done up large bath-attached bedroom. After mother and I die, this house, it has told me, hopes to be knocked down by prospective buyers wall by wall, brick by brick, curtain rod by curtain rod and a new house, a happy house, to come up here in its place. This room, this bed, under which I had often hid as a child, will be dismantled, the fears that bleached me to the bone will be no more. Not even in the remotest corner of someone's farthest memory. My darkness will extinguish with me.

For now. For now it was me on this bed tossing, on this bed turning. Hopeful and hopeless. When a brand new soul enters my cryonically frozen body in a hi-tech lab far into the future, will I come back to life calling out, 'Kumar'?

Inexplicable what remains when we move on, what missing is made up of each time we miss. Yes, I missed him—despite my fuckingest not to—and idly contemplated what would happen if I voiced this compulsion to him, to see him always, to cuddle him, to hold hands, to put my head on his chest, my ear to his heart. His after-laugh, the little echo of a laugh that follows his real laugh, as if in appreciation of the laugh just laughed. The look in his eye that steams me open, like my thoughts are spiral staircases for him to climb. His open-mouth kisses that suck my soul up a straw…

Good God, what next? His lint in my navel? But even as I snigger, a hand surreptitiously, without my sanction, reaches out for the phone. I look down, it is in my hand! I throw it against the wall with all my might. *Shh. Tongue, don't say them, those words are drunk.*

Point to be noted, milord, such words are terminally ill; even as you say them they die. Or a pathological lie, said to flatter and fool, if not a fatal gunshot; sorry, send your body where?

I am not mad at anyone. No one owes me anything. I mean, who *are* they? I have to remember again and again and again my innate gift for turning people away. At the back of my mouth a rotting tooth stinks up my sweetest word. If Kumar hadn't left me today, he would have left me tomorrow. Like this man had, like that man had. Like all men do.

It is always night outside when a man calls it a day deep inside you. I am fine by myself, fuck you very much.

Chapter 9

The timing couldn't have been more right. The house help passed away without further ado; it seems she had a lump in her breast not benign in the least. Her son-in-law came here, telling me all the symptoms in great detail, as if I was an oncologist, though ma lay back and listened to the list, even made him repeat a few, with a contented look, diverting his tendency to break into Tulu, a local dialect, with well-timed grunts. I felt my so-called convent-educated superior status wrap me like cling film, and paid him not just her due salary but something I calculated would cover the funeral costs. To tell the truth, I had nothing much to do with her, and was guilty of holding my breath whenever she passed me by, though I watched hawk-like each time she reported for work to check if she washed her hands with the cheap antiseptic soap I kept out for her.

Mother insisted we go to see the body, so off we went. A quick path was cut for us through the crowd and the mourners fell silent, as they stopped looking at the deceased and turned to look at us. The son-in-law came to us and spoke in broken English, 'Ambulance out, she out,' like we might think some part of her had still not made it to her own funeral.

His wife, who had been relaxing on a stool by the body and chatting away to relatives, got up as we approached and began to wail loudly. With a quick eye-roll she summoned her two daughters too to wail by her side. I tried to look grief-stricken but couldn't quite pull it off. Muniamma dead looked more alive than she had ever done before, lying there in what must have been her bridal finery, right down to a large faux gold nose-ring that would have cut off her oxygen had she been breathing. The daughter and her two daughters continued to wail and I knew they couldn't stop till we left (it wouldn't look nice), but we had just reached and couldn't leave immediately (it wouldn't look nice). The granddaughters occasionally wandered off or brought the volume of wails down but with a click of her tongue or furious blinks from their mother were summoned to the job at hand—mourning. One murmured she was hungry, and her mother gave her an I-will-kill-you-and-feed-you-to-you look. And I thought, god, how much of mothering and daughtering were shows put up for others.

*

'Calm down, Eeedee. Tell me again what happened.'

'Someone knows. I am telling you someone knows.'

'We go through this, you know that. We go through this all the time. We feel followed. We feel overheard. We feel watched. It is okay, that is our life.'

She took a loud breath and I could hear her exhale all the way here. 'It is not that. Don't patronize me. I got a call.'

'A call?' I wound the landline's wire tight around my index finger. 'What did they say?'

'No one spoke. But Rudra!' When I said nothing, she added, 'Calls. Not call. Someone is calling me up every bloody day. You are not listening to me!'

'True caller ID?'

'Says spam number. No actual number comes up, some gibberish with a lot of x and z.'

'So there you have it.'

'Why would someone spam-call me exactly at three a.m. every day? You tell me that.'

'Complain to the police.'

'Are you sure? Rudra, be sure of what you say. Do you want the police in?'

No, I didn't but I had occupied the conventional land of non-secrets, or at least been traversing a man-woman land of not-so-secret secrets that hurt and harm no one, long enough so that this intrusion of my life as it really was did not begin to make sense.

'Let me think this over and call you tomorrow. Meanwhile switch off your mobile for the night.'

I went to the window and looked out. Any moment now I feared I would hear Eeedee's voice. Not this one, the adult one that spoke on the phone so diffidently. But the other one, the one that came from a six-year-old Ela.

*

Life until four years of age had been a blur. Papa travelled a lot, ma waited for him a lot, and I was Ayah's bitter business. She told me how she had to leave behind her own little babies to come and look after me, because I could not pick up after myself, feed myself, bathe myself, dress myself. 'And your mother? Don't get me started,' she said in a dialect I learnt automatically and spoke better than my mother tongue. And though the storeroom next to the kitchen was her designated quarters, she'd be in my bed between really late at night and really early in the morning, pushing me into the farthest corner of my own bed. Late in the night she muttered into my ear what sounded like specially composed curses not just for me but all my ancestors, like a lullaby sung backward. I clung to her though, she was all I knew. Every time she hit me, she made me feel special later. I knew if I ever tried to tell ma about this unique treatment at Ayah's hands, ma would disbelieve me or sack Ayah; both options were not appealing, not at the age I was, not yet four.

And there was the business of bed-wetting, mine not hers, which she minded acutely as my pee travelled to her. It was not just the wetness that woke me up but her whack right there, sometimes mid-pee.

At times during dinner I caught her eye and would stop what I was about to say, because when ma and papa were away in the evening, for movies or dinners or where their gaiety took them, she would have a lot to say about anything I had said. She'd box me where no one could see. Clots spread their dark wings like moths on my inner thighs and upper arms in hidden flesh folds after she pinched me with her sharp nails.

It was only when watery bubbles broke out all over Ayah's skin and it turned out to be chicken pox that she was sent home for two weeks. Briefly, too briefly, I was the apple of my parents' eyes, in what was the interval of the long movie of my life, we were free to play family-family. Papa plucked me out of anonymity and filled my mind with myriad images, from books, such beautiful books. They were a confused collage of shimmer and rouge, foreign phrases and magic beans, stars that refused to twinkle unless I called out to them. When Ayah came back everything almost went back to how it had been. Except that a little girl happened to all of us and it wasn't me.

Papa's colleague, a widower called Dr Dhar, died in a car accident and he had left behind a child, Ela. There was some uncle, an eccentric bachelor of no fixed timetable and hence unsuitable as guardian for her. Talk both shushed and furious between my parents went on for a while and then suddenly a radical decision was taken; Ela would stay with us till she completed school. There was a trust fund that would take care of her financial needs, but the family she was to get was us: papa, ma and me.

My parents came at me in a chorus. 'You are going to get a sister.'

Ayah went ballistic with rage. She pulled my hair, continuously hit the top of my head with her fist as if hammering me smaller and let loose a string of abuse. 'As if looking after one child is not enough! Pay me double I say! Your mother should never have had a child. Does she look at you twice? But ugly children are unwanted children. Not your mother's fault. She is okay looking, so is your father, but you? Who has seen an uglier child? The first time I saw you…'

I switched off. I had heard all this before. The first time she saw me she had fainted, my plainness had knocked her unconscious. Yeah yeah yeah. But a girl roughly my own age was coming! I couldn't get over this news. Somehow I knew my life was going to change. That Ela was going to be the one to love me. No one had fallen in love with me yet, but all that was over now. I was going to be loved and I was going to love.

When she arrived the first thing I noted was Ela had swollen eyes. From a lack of sleep and crying. Maybe her Ayah had been rough on her too, I thought. Suddenly I had a purpose. Taking the newcomer under my wing, seeing to her comfort, giving her company all the time kept me on my toes. I saw more of ma and a lot more of papa than I used to. It was as if Ela had brought us all together. We were invited out a lot, everyone wanted to see the orphan child. And we took her around with such élan. It never once occurred to me to be jealous. I only watched keenly as the dark circles under her eyes disappeared, the eyelids went back to normal and she slowly lost that bewildered look. My parents were featured in a newspaper—a photographer came home and clicked pictures of them with Ela on the swing— and people were always telling them how kind they were.

'You are really my sister?' Ela would ask, snuggling up to me in bed at night. Though we had been given different rooms, she invariably shared mine after the adults had gone to sleep.

'I can't be your brother.' I'd hug her tight and stroke her back. And when she slept, I slept. She was older, but I was bigger. If we were sisters, she was the little sister.

We went to school together, Ayah holding both our hands. At lunch break we would find each other through the maze of classes and sit under a tree in school, eating the same snack packed from the same home.

No one knows why adults take certain decisions, and that too with such surgical precision. One night we went to bed semi-sisters, the next morning we were told that from now on we would have nothing to do with each other, nothing. To begin with, she was shifted to a different school, a government one with minimal fees. The Ayah was now wholly mine again; she was told to look after me and only me. Ela made her own plaits, and did her own homework. Ma helped only with mine. There were fruits for me, tall glasses of milk and chocolates through the day. For her there was a tardy cup of no-milk tea and some cheap biscuits once a day.

Though the decision to accord us separate statuses— have and have-not—was taken at the top level and I had nothing to do with it, Ela turned away from me too.

'She is nobody to us,' my mother said to me again and again and I am not sure Ela did not hear her. I am not sure ma did not mean Ela not to hear her. Ayah was less mean to me as she had found a new target in Ela. Ela had to hear over and over again about her ill luck, her unlucky stars and her black, black fate.

My fifth birthday was coming up and there was to be a party, which was an occasion to return all those other birthday parties I went to as far as ma was concerned. She sat at the dining table holding her head in her hands with a sullen look, clamping down tight on any animation on my part, saying, *oh, we have to do this* in doomed groans. Cake in the shape of a squirrel with white and dark chocolate stripes (I was going through an 'I want to be a vet' phase, but thought nothing of gobbling up make-believe fauna. Ela said nothing when asked what would she be when she grew up; she said she did not believe she would grow up. How I laughed! '*Everyone* grows up, stupid.'), candles that wouldn't go off however much you blew and blew, potato chips, ice cream and return gifts! All of which was driving ma to despair.

Still, I was getting excited. The night before my birthday after everyone had gone to sleep, I crept into Ela's room; the storeroom originally Ayah's. Ayah, demoted, now slept in the corridor on the floor and her snores shook the whole house.

'Ela,' I whispered.

But what was this? In Ela's bed was papa. Under him, she. Lying so still, her eyes open, all white.

'Papa!' I said. But he jumped up with such fury that I shrank. Also, he was naked. I had never seen him naked. Never. This frightened me more. (Where were his clothes? Wasn't he feeling cold?) More than him cuddling Ela when he should be cuddling me, his daughter. She was someone else's child. Surely I was entitled to any hugs and kisses he had to give.

'Roo,' he said and the menace in his voice disconcerted me.

Instinctively I ducked. I ran back to my room, his footsteps sounded just behind me. I crept under my bed. And there I shivered all night. I shouldn't have gone to Ela's room at night. I shouldn't have disobeyed my parents. But underneath my fear was a more basic, fundamental question: what had papa been doing in that bed?

I did not venture out to Ela's room ever again. I stayed in my own bed. Lying unmoving on it or hidden under it I heard papa's unmistakable voice, full of such rich affection, saying Ela's name in a strange way, not the way he said it during the day. This was another way, with an indescribable sweetness, as if her name on it melted his tongue.

I am not sure when and how I realized the true nature of papa's nightly hugs, but etched in my memory is a day out with ma when we had both stepped out of the house and I looked back to see papa stand there holding Ela by her hand and her looking at us with such bleak eyes. In those eyes, as an adult now I know, I sensed an entire accusation, a premature knowledge of life and a total lack of hope. At the time I only remember asking ma on our way to my dance class, 'Why is Ela always so sad?'

'Her parents are dead. Did you forget?'

So that's how Ela grew up in my house, as the Girl Whose Parents Were Dead. I don't know who I was. Perhaps a hastily drawn girl on the wall of a public loo, shady phone number scribbled by the side, 'call for a good time'. Two large circles for boobs and a large V for crotch. You know, the kind pubescent boys with breaking voices come up with when they feel… artsy.

No one loved me and I loved no one. It just turned out that way.

*

That's not to say Ela and I did not form a bond of our own. Arriving at friendship from the other end, the speed of dark the same as speed of light, 299,792 kilometres per second.

'Take this.' Early on, I handed her my favourite book. *Little Women*. It was the only book I possessed, the only book I loved back then. My first book her first book.

At night I alone heard the bed creak, that muted sob, the indrawn breath. Ma, with her sleeping pills and headaches, retired early in a haze of eucalyptus, loudly alluding to papa's nocturnal need to raid his own library. This is what she told stray guests who came home, how papa was always referencing and annotating and 'preparing for next day's class' late at night or early in the morning, to explain away to herself his absence in their bed when she went to sleep and when she woke up. I lay in the dark straining to hear. Listening. To the gaps between the bed creaks. His grunt, her mewl. It became a habit, to huddle under the bed and dream of sleep, to wait for nights to be darker, absolute, to smother and suffocate. But no night could manage the black I demanded. Even as my days grew night-coloured.

*

Ayah's stories meanwhile began to flesh out, in her telling and now in my prepubescent understanding of them. Her bedtime tales. When all of her life lived until now was crushed like so many bitter pills on her tongue for her to swallow. The husband who never married her. (My husband, she called him, and then went on about how he never had the guts to stand by her, hold her hand and make her his wife, as he already had a wife who lived with his mother. I am confused still about the exact details of her legally wedded status but the teary anger spilling from her never escaped me for a moment.) The children she bore that were scattered with relatives she had to pay till she died. The rich-rich officer man who hired her because his wife was 'ill and indisposed', and whom she had to leave in the end because 'taking off my clothes every night and lying next to a man who does nothing, is that life? What do I get out of that?'

One unremarkable morning, just like that, Ayah was dismissed. She had said something unpalatable to ma and ma dealt with her in her own way, by throwing her out overnight. Tin box in hand, looking dressy in one of ma's old saris, she cried what ma called crocodile tears. And though I had mixed feelings about her exit, I also knew anything I uttered in her favour would be held against her. The house was constricted enough as it was, its walls growing closer, squeezing everyone in it into smaller spaces, and Ayah's departure at some level, I presumed, would free up air for the rest of us.

Her going only made the family unit tighter, kneaded us that much closer to each other into a ball of dough no outsider could penetrate, the silences that fell between us now denser. With no eyes on us, our breaths were going through each other's chests. The maids who came in after that too disinterested and temporary to obey mother's elaborate partiality system, where one child got ghee on her parathas and almond paste in her milk as birthright and the other made do with dry rotis and water. Ela's beds and mine were now made by a blinder eye, an eye that saw no reason not to match the Mickey Mouse and Snow White motifs of our sheets. I remember one of these maids coming out with a threadbare sheet, a staple on Ela's bed, laughing. 'Memsaab, ye toh mujhe bhi nahi chahiye!'

How many times could ma—who had other things to worry about like losing her looks, which she tried to repair day and night with imported creams and homemade concoctions, and frequent food-poisoning which I now think were half-hearted suicide bids— keep reminding the indifferent one-hour maids of my privileged status in the household? Since the elevation bestowed on me had only been power play on her part rather than a motherly fit, its passing went unnoticed.

Then ma began to baby the house. New curtains, new cushions, new paintings on newly painted walls, anything to recapture the magic of her bygone heydays. She also started to cook and meal times became painful elaborate sit-downs with napkins on laps where she pretended Ela and I were two sisters seated on one side of the table, while she sat with her husband on the other, together, a pair, a couple. 'I have cooked this with my own hands,' became her anthem, recited with whatever she served, as if there was a lesser known method of cooking with feet. This manic cooking spree was interrupted, first rarely and then more and more frequently, by no cooking, so that bread had to be bought last minute from the corner shop if it wasn't shut that late in the day and each member of the family learnt to staunch his or her own hunger in his or her own way. I boiled eggs, Ela scrambled them or the other way round. Papa ate them the way she made them, regardless of the eggs being scrambled, fried, boiled or curried. No one, least of all me, went to ma's room and asked her why she wasn't cooking, why she wasn't eating.

She said she bled buckets, there was a hysterectomy much against her wishes, her howling cries to avoid it and the hormone therapy that thinned her hair, gave her acne and ape-like fuzz. Funny what those two can do to you, progesterone and oestrogen.

One night she barged into my room—it happened only on this one occasion—showing me a chain, completely ballistic, saying something garbled about it being gold, real gold, drooling and stuttering, so that I turned to the wall and continued to sleep. Really, jewellery, now or then, never moved the earth for me.

I was twelve and Ela nearly fifteen when we finally knew what we must do. It came upon us as a fully formed plan of action though at the time we did not recognize it as such, our thoughts in sync without the need for eye contact. I was plump, with paws for hands, and she was scrawny with the same puffy eyelids she first came with. All bones, with eyes that stuck out like ribs—elbows, knees, the long line of transparent spine that clicked as she walked.

It was the night they had a fight. Ela and papa. It was the night ma came out of her room, because she could not sleep despite the pills. It was the night I got a cricket bat home.

I was sports captain by default; it wasn't a post anyone wanted. Since the sports room was locked and the key was with the PT sir who had left early for the day, the bat couldn't be left out for anyone to steal. Hence, the bat was sent with me for safe-keeping until the next day.

Loud voices woke me up. Ela was sobbing and papa was chortling. He was drunk that night too, like all other nights. 'My rani, my nanhi rani,' he kept saying.

Ela screamed, something crashed to the ground and then ma was howling at the top of her voice that Ela was a slut who had seduced her husband. Papa was trying to go down on a knee—he kept toppling over at each attempt, unbalanced by his potbelly—saying, 'will you marry me?' to Ela. He loved her, he said, like he had never loved, like no one had ever loved. He pointed at ma, saying, 'Not her. Never her.' Now ma sobbed, tears wriggling like fat worms down her cheeks, her mouth hanging open as if something was stuck in her windpipe. The third-person 'her' instead of the more personal 'you' hit her harder than the rest.

When I came into Ela's tiny room, papa was trying to put his arms around her middle, more for support, and she was disappearing into herself, growing gaunter and gaunter, literally pared down to a pair of popping eyes by a long-time lack of nourishment, in a bid to escape the embrace. A man's love can leave you skeletal, vacuum the marrow out of your bones.

I went back to my room, returned with the bat and raised it high.

'Let her go,' I ordered him.

He turned to me with rabid eyes. There was no fondness, not the slightest recollection of our blood tie, just a deep hatred culled exclusively for me. Still kneeling, he didn't leave her as I bade and I had to bring down the bat on his head. Once, twice, thrice. Till blood gushed and his head pulped. And still I brought the bat down.

Ela helped me wash my hands and then she made us some tea. I kept sipping the tea and vomiting. I could never touch tea again. Green, yes. Black, at a pinch. But sugary milky tea, no, never. I cannot forget how it all curdled at the bottom of my throat.

Ma, Ela and I sat with heads bowed, in the drawing room, silently, our eyes fixed away from the room where papa lay on the floor with his head smashed. Occasionally we took a peek and looked away, shuddering.

We made up a story about intruders and the police bought it. Because look at us, two chits of girls, with our fatherless, naked faces defencelessly turned to the macho protective men in uniform. Mother would pass out routinely under questioning, and Ela and I would back each other up on what happened. And our story never changed.

Chapter 10

Ela left soon, it was for the best. In the days before she left there were such scenes, as each one of us went through some breakdown or the other; mother poured some mild acid kept to clean toilets into her eyes and lost partial sight, Ela repeated over and over again that her diary was stolen, the one in which she had recorded all of the atrocities borne by her and now was possibly in enemy hands, and I? I got the giggles.

Actually, ma had intended to drink up the stuff and kill herself, like in the movies. She would dwindle, she thought, and fade, and be no more, like a light shower that leaves the clouds, with a dab of petrichor on her inner wrist like mild perfume. But the melodrama of her action, the logistics of actually staging her own suicide, overwhelmed her, made her hands shake, and instead of going smoothly down her throat the acid flecked her face. Drops fell into her eyes, irreversibly damaging her cornea, and if she smiles too wide there are holes in her gums. Ophthalmologists were flummoxed by this unique 'accident'; her sight was restored sixty percent, owing to the spurious nature and low degree of the bleach-acid component in the cleaning liquid and mother's own shaky hand, faltering in the middle of such an empty grand gesture. 'Sati or what?' like her sister asked. My aunt left soon after this incident, but from then on has been coming every year to give me a break, as she says, but also to keep ma's melodrama in check. A drama queenery that meant she could no longer read her women's magazines, despite the new thick glasses, but could still somewhat make out the happenings on a large TV screen. It was possible to escape her attention—as the maids and I found out eventually—if one stood unmoving before her long enough. Just like she had long involved conversations with a billowing curtain or an indoor plant, mistaking it for one of us.

On the day of the funeral they brought a beauty-parloured papa, all shaved and over-perfumed, in his wedding suit straight from the mortuary and arranged him carefully like a rambling centrepiece in the front room. A floral profusion followed, bouquets began to wilt and wither in the afternoon heat, their fragrance a bit off—do flowers fart?

Someone, with a hand at the back of my head, forced me to bend down and kiss his cheek. I looked at him properly then. His eyes were shut, not accusingly fixed on me as I had expected, and I realized for the first time that this man looked so much like me. Or, as everyone else put it, I looked so much like this man.

Caught in flagrante delicto by death. None of that embarrassment on his face though. His features relaxed along lines my own features would blunt out into with age, with wear and tear, with wanting what cannot be wanted over the years, and being thwarted at every want. My future mouth, my future chin. So did I have his past mouth and chin? I began to grope my face blindly, frantically, feeling ill, till someone held my hands tightly in their own.

They asked me to say something to him. My last words. A farewell. I stalled indefinitely but when they stopped insisting and turned away from me, I decided to quote his precious Shakespeare back to him, '*Why should a dog, a horse, a rat have life, and thou no breath at all?*' A rhetorical question, the only kind you ask the dead.

I kept switching on the radio. FM songs played loudly and then someone would come and switch it off. I would switch it right back on. Lata Mangeshkar's coy declarations of love and then silence. Kishore Kumar's lament of never finding a soulmate and then silence. Weather report, a stray headline, static and then silence. This went on till someone hid the radio, and then silence. This, more than anything else—the sombre faces of everyone, the exaggerated praise of papa from total strangers, the black tea from the neighbour's house that everyone declined or sipped with distaste like papa had made it himself in the process of dying, and the bat that I kept in the sewage-filled gutter behind our house where slum kids came to defecate—got to me. First I hid my smile behind a hand, then I put both hands to my mouth, but my smile kept growing larger and larger till it leaked all over my face. I laughed and I laughed, still guffawing as they led me away, the poor, fatherless mite, whose grief was coming out all wrong. They had to sedate me; some good doctor brought out a syringe and went for my arm.

And then silence.

When I woke up the next day the funeral was over. Eeedee lay next to me. 'They had to cut his coat top to bottom at the back to make it fit,' she said solemnly and I was uncontrollably laughing again. The idea of seeing him from the back, as he lay gravely, impeccably deceased, with his coat cut into two behind him was too much. I began to hiccup and choke, tears streaming down my face, laughing uproariously all over again, hitting my thigh, holding my sides, so that Eeedee got the others and someone slapped me. But the more they slapped the more it looked to me like a Charlie Chaplin movie. I could not feel the slaps, only see them. It was decided that no one would talk to me or set me off on this unbecoming merriment. Even today if someone says 'coat' I burst into loud shivering laughs.

A student of papa's came home with a large well-packed rectangle under his armpit and we watched silently curious as he unwrapped it. What emerged was a gilt-framed photo of papa. Almost full length, papa was dressed in a black blazer with his prestigious alma mater's initials on its lapel, an alma mater he managed to mention in every conversation he ever had, looking straight at the camera, which meant he could find you and follow you with his eyes wherever you were in the room.

When the student hung it on the wall (he came prepared with nails and hammer), we tried our best not to show our surprise. He stepped back and all of us looked at the photo, very much like a photo ourselves. The boy hung back at the door, puzzled, I think, by the lack of a thank you from any one of us. He thought us mad and we thought him mad, each of us an emperor reigning over our independent lunacies.

Papa still hangs on the wall. During power cuts at night

I have sometimes caught ma addressing it in sing-song, maybe what was her honeymoon voice. 'You,' she says and stops, then starts again, 'you'. Then comes the hand-wringing, the whining, the should-be and the could-be. But during the day when I am about, no one, including her, looks at the photo. The maids dust everything but this, as no one has ever pulled them up for it. Behind the frame, as a result, are old spider colonies and dust enough to form another earth.

Life kills is all we need to know about living. Slowly, one day at a time, we die without being able to say this is how I died, this is what death felt like, looked like. But ask for death and life looks you in the eye, and slowly, so slowly, lingers over you.

*

Of course, I had the diary, the diary that killed me and delivered me into this lifeless life, this diary that's cyanide on my tongue, with its words I can never quote, a knowledge I can never share, words that will die with me. I cannot tell anyone what it tastes of. I had known about its existence from the day she started writing it. From the day she entered our house. I had only wanted to know her better, my intentions had been honourable. That day, after we disposed of the bat and called the police, I picked it up, sure that it would give us away; I knew even then that I was the only one twisted enough to carry this off. I quite intended to mulch it, but just never got around to doing it, I guess. And the possibility of this diary floating about the stratosphere occasionally panicked her. From time to time, she had an attack like this, when she was sure someone was blackmailing her, and then she'd just be a high-pitched voice at the end of a phone. The rest of the time she was, like me, a model citizen.

After she left our home for good, she never came back. It was an unspoken pact between her and ma. Ela went to college in some city far away and I here in my hometown. We both studied English; my father had infected us with his love for language. We both loved crosswords, European literature, puns, etymology and wordplay. We both hoarded books like cobblers did nails. We discussed (on phone, in letters, in person) characters in novels like they were people we knew and had grown up with. And we both sniffed the books we gave each other.

*

Two days after that phone call Eeedee was back in the house she had sworn never to set foot in again.

It was not her return so much as her not having warned me of it that surprised me. Of course, she was welcome to come and go as she pleased; ma for all her posturing knew what was what even when the what had been going on right under her nose. But to land up like this, unannounced with bags, out of the blue, seemed not her usual style.

Still, the pleasure of setting eyes on her overrode the abruptness of her arrival.

After dinner she brought up the diary—again. 'I wrote it all down as it happened, and I remember each and every word I wrote. In fact, I can't forget a single word! Anyone who reads it will know we did it, Roo.'

I looked back at her steadily. 'If we cannot find the diary, after such copious searching, how can anyone else? Tell me that.'

'*Someone* has it. It can't just vanish into thin air. It had three hundred pages, that blasted diary.'

Hardly a hundred, I wanted to correct her, but let her exaggerate the number of its pages and her fears. Anything to let her vent out the dread.

'As long as it is out there, I cannot sleep.'

'If you are determined to not see reason, Eeedee darling, there is little I can do to interfere.'

She waved a helpless hand. 'You are in the clear…'

'In the clear? *In the clear?* I killed him! I am the one

who should shake like a leaf at the slightest sound and never sleep till I die.'

'Shh,' she said, gathering me to her, my head on her heart.

I knew this was the best way to shut her up, remind her of my guilt, my role in it. She was only the victim, I was a coldblooded murderer.

'And no more of those anonymous calls, I hope. I told you—'

'No, no, I forgot to tell you. That guy finally spoke, and you were so right, I was getting worked up for nothing. The line hadn't been clear, you know how the network is at my place. It was just a wrong number in the end. Some guy who kept asking me how I knew about his wife. What wife, boss, I kept asking him. He just kept asking me so many questions! But this made me think, maybe there is money in starting a detective agency. We only have to tail a lot of married couples and find out who they are sleeping with. What do you say, Roo?'

I mumbled a fake-scandalized 'whaaaat?' but was too busy trying not to compulsively re-read the message I had just gotten from Kumar.

Thinking of you and how you stopped talking to me and how I can't stop thinking of you since you stopped talking to me and the time I asked if I am talking too much and you said don't stop.

Why didn't I delete it—this message—on arrival?

This was reading material and I will read anything, okay? But beautiful short stories on my phone do not move me too much. Alone in bed, a bottle in hand, monogamy is gibberish. Wailing for demon-lover. Once? Twice? Then you are, like, take me, someone. Anyone.

Someone somewhere is making his way to me and I have to keep myself free for him. He will see my side profile and be intrigued, maddened, by my lack of awareness of him, of his desire, though that desire is dependent for its survival on precisely that unawareness and once I am aware and face him squarely and respond with a desire of my own then it is time for him to hunt for another face, another desire, and time for someone else to watch my profile. I will not respond to random sporadic texts, I will not. I would rather cut off my fingers than text him back. Instead I will wait like a good little girl for another man to find my flaws beautiful, to offer to suture all my gaping holes. For the perfect man to find me perfect.

No way will I inform Kumar that his silence gave me earache.

*

Mother asked me how long 'my friend' was going to stay. In a voice of steel I said, 'As long as she wants. Why do you care? You will die soon.'

She said nothing for a while, then, 'You are a fool. You are my own flesh and blood, but a fool all the same.'

I pretended to wipe away a tear. 'Oh no, my own mother doesn't love me. Woe is me etc. This butter hasn't melted at all. When did you take it out of the fridge? You cannot wait till it is time for me to go to school to keep it on the table! This is like trying to spread stone on bread!'

Even as I tossed the butter bowl to the ground, ma was away in ma world. 'He'd get so mad,' she confided brightly, her head bobbing as if a ponytail was still attached to it, 'if I didn't tell him I love him thrice a day. Can you imagine! I had so much to do…' Here her voice trailed off, no doubt trying to locate in her feeble memory a single job executed by her. 'Mathematicians can be lovers, yes, but are lovers mathematicians?'

If it wasn't about papa's love for literature, it was about her long-ago procured degree in maths. Before I left I had one important job: shift the diary to where it couldn't be found. Which I did. I took it with me to school and put it in the locker assigned to me. There it was, next to the letters papa wrote to Eeedee, his nanhi jaan, nanhi pari, and in one instance, nanhi nanhi. I had found these too, among his papers, his posthumous paeans of love. And they were in Hindi because Ela spoke more Hindi than English when she first came to us. Sometime during her stay, perhaps coinciding with his grand passion for her, he banned ma and me from colloquial Bangla at home, a diktat we still adhered to, speaking in English when we had to, but mostly getting away speaking nothing at all.

Some days I sit in the staffroom poring over these letters of his. Except for the endearments, the letters were written in flowery English, a pompous version of English that is the preserve of swooning swains. I have memorized every word. I know the exact sequence of sentences, where he gets his spellings in a knot, a man who was proud of his mastery over the language. There are words he has written and then cut out. I exhume them. From obsolete ink, the corpse of a script. There are words scratched out so much that I cannot read them, with nothing salvageable. These words obsess me, so that I take hours to come up with alternative words, to second-guess my dad the lover, the poet, my late, late non-dad dad. A netherworld crossword. And when I get a word right, sometimes in the middle of the night in the middle of my sleep, I sit up straight, hand to throat, choking. Demons grab me by the hair then, my bones powdering in their guttural grip. The power to unforget, who has that? To unsee, to unhear? Your retina has photocopy machines you know nothing about. I mean, what does one do with the CCTV inside the head? Don't we all sit up nights rubbing back and forth the blisters on our skins with a compulsive finger? No browser history is ever deleted. Ever. It is all there, daring you to double click.

And the diary. It was a sacred text, each entry in it talismanic, a prayer prayed. It consisted of a will to live, to forgive, to make it from one day to the next. It chronicled live pain. It was what happened. I needed it in my hand, before my eyes, to match the words in my head to it. Words I saw clearly, heard clearly, and came back again and again to check if I was right, if I was wrong. Not that I thought these things with too clear a mind; I only knew there was no way I could, even if I wanted to, wipe it out. If I did that, maybe I was scared, it would become just another story I had heard while growing up.

'Can I bother you for a moment?'

I looked up.

It was the formerly immoral teacher who was now back after her suspension.

Don't talk too much, I ordered myself, just keep your mouth shut, and all will be fine. Since I was the one who had informed her husband—using Eeedee's phone during my vacation—about her extramarital outing, I had reason to quake in my shoes. After listening to her conduct her affair on her phone in what she thought a discreet manner but was for me flagrantly intrusive, I grew tired; tired of being invisible, of simply not being there just because I was childless and my ring finger bare, as if I had somehow turned into a eunuch and was deaf and dumb to boot. I wanted to put my shoe into her mouth and stamp out her secret-most giggle. Also, in my defence, I was bored. So somehow I had gotten hold of her landline, and dialled it until a male voice finally answered. I had apprised him with a vowel-less speed of his cuckold status. Who, who, he kept asking, as if I knew or cared about the lover, as if her sleeping with the president of the United States may make it all right. Only later it occurred to me he probably meant who was speaking, as in who was I.

Now as his wife advanced towards me, she appeared to know that it had been me who made that call; I prepared to die.

'It was so difficult to track you down, ma'am!' she said. 'We just found out that it is you who called my husband from somewhere in Tamil Nadu. And,' she put a hand on my shoulder before I could jump back in time, 'I want to thank you from the bottom of my heart. That man,' she made a gagging sound, 'that man I loved... I thought we would marry and he just… just vanished! He never loved me. But my husband is a gem of a man. He took me back without a word.' She stared at me with her face watering all over—eyes, nose, mouth. 'You have a heart of gold. If you hadn't told him, this day would never have come. Because of you, ma'am, my eyes are now opened! That guy would never have married me, never have stood by me… What an idiot I was to almost throw away everything I had! And you made me see that. You! *How can I ever thank you?*' Overcome once again, she hugged me tight. The staffroom was empty, but the peon who had come to collect the empty teacups no doubt thought she was starting a torrid affair with me.

I stiffly told her she was mistaken and that neither had I any idea about who she was sleeping with nor had I any interest in disengaging her lower half from one person and reattaching it to another. Nothing more disturbing than having your bitchiest act treated as saintly.

Back home over dinner I casually asked Eeedee if she had inadvertently given her spam caller my details. For a moment she looked stricken, then she said lightly enough that she was so petrified by those calls, she couldn't remember what she had said or not said to them. 'I think that they asked if I knew anyone here, in this town. I don't know why they asked this, but I don't remember mentioning you either. I think… I really cannot remember. Why do you ask?'

'Nothing,' I said, 'I just got a silent call myself.'

*

From that night ma took to bed, perhaps to protest against Eeedee's reappearance in her territory. She stopped eating and she stopped talking, except for the occasional babble about her bridal days and, nauseatingly for us, nights.

'This won't do,' I scolded her. 'You have to get out of bed at least to go to the bathroom.' Eeedee got some adult diapers and together we secured them around ma. Who despite looking bird-like weighed a ton. Cleaning her and dressing her were all we seemed to be doing at home, though I must say Eeedee's willingness, especially at night, to take care of ma surprised and relieved me. Together, with her timely ablutions and my rigid going through the motions, we made up one half-hearted Florence Nightingale between us.

'You have just come back from school,' she'd excuse me. Or 'You have to go to school now.'

Ma's room began to smell of shit however painstakingly, nitpickingly, we cleaned her. I tried not to breathe in the room so that when I walked out it was like suffering an asthma attack. My clothes too began to smell of her shit. The food we ate, the air we breathed, everything came straight from ma's bowels. Sometimes I saw her play with her own faeces. Pick it and examine it closely like some new toy. It was left to Eeedee and me to clean it from her fingernails, from her hair.

And the prattle! When it came, it came in unstoppable torrents. All addressed to her dead husband. Naked outpourings of devotion. Inarticulate entreaties and coquettish laughs, like a kitten lived on her tongue. From a pre-widowhood, pre-betrayal era, every orifice lax. She'd sit up thrilled, energized by what ran through her mind. Eeedee and I would stand by awkwardly, waiting for the fit to be over. For her to lapse into blessed silence, to be packed back into bed. And as we left, we'd ignore the odd smacks and slurps from her. It was something you wanted to flee from—the old slamming gums in memory of desire.

The school became my solace, the place to escape to. And though I felt sorry leaving Eeedee behind with the bulk of ma-related chores, I stopped protesting when she said, 'It is all right. I feel I owe her.'

In my mind I was a generous sort, lending her my mother as she had none. I'd wake multiple times in a single night because Eeedee was either getting into or out of bed while tending to ma, and when she wasn't there, when she was in ma's room, I only thought of what a nuisance it was to not sleep in a straight stretch. I had half a mind to ask her to move into ma's room.

*

The staffroom could get like this once in a blue moon, like the inside of a grave. I was enjoying this humanless calm before the door was pushed open and in came two storms—the formerly immoral but now moral with a vengeance teacher and a morally neither here nor there teacher, both intensely discussing their dream cake. First they praised each other's baking, and addressed most of the fulsome twittering to me as if I was referee. My unfortunate seating in the centre meant I had to nod at strategic points in their conversation. 'Give me that curd cake recipe,' begged the second one and the first, after much cajoling, coyly parted with it. The asker wrote it all down carefully and left for her next class, thanking the other profusely. The recipe-giver went and shut the door firmly after her and came to me with measured steps. I wondered if I should scream for help. She had been stopped mid-mating by me, she may want to kill me, right?

She looked at me a longish while before confiding in all seriousness, 'I haven't given her the secret ingredient, but to you I shall.' She leaned over and whispered in my ear, 'Mixed fruit jam,' even though there was no one in the room except Mahatma Gandhi and Jawaharlal Nehru on the wall, their smiles never dimming at this slight. Now I wished I had listened to the recipe instead of merely pretending that I had. I will just have to get together with the other teacher and bake the perfect cake one day. We will meet in black overcoats in a back alley and I will psst in her ears… what? I forget.

After particularly restless nights ma could sleep like a baby till noon. Eeedee and I went for a morning walk to the stadium. Here, despite never having told her about Kumar, I had to introduce him to her as there he was in his sneakers, trying his best, I am sure, to bump into me. It would be silly to look through someone whom you had known intimately, whose body you Brailled with eyes closed in the middle of many a midnight.

'Hello.'

Good to hear his stupid voice again. 'Hi,' I said, 'Meet my friend, Ela.'

'Ela,' he said, shaking her hand, his eyes going over her face in slow motion. Serpents spat and hissed in me.

'She is just visiting us. She has this happening dress shop near Ooty…'

'I shut it,' she said abruptly.

Baffled, I turned to her. She hadn't told me that. 'But why?'

'It was totally in the red, that's why.' She shrugged. 'There was no point going on with it really.' Flashing Kumar a sunny smile, 'We bookworms can't read the bottomline.'

He laughed and she laughed. I laughed too, if a tad late. That was not funny. That was… come-hither.

As we walked back home neither of us said anything about the man we met. I had to rush for school, hoping to reach there before the bell. The principal was an affable woman but even she would be hard put to condone too many late-comings in a row.

At night Eeedee and I read silently, the only sound in the room that of our pages turning. Ma had been given her sleeping pills, what she had been taking for years, and which we had discontinued in the wake of her recent degeneration. Eeedee and I had a light dinner and were enjoying just stretching our backs. I looked up; something was amiss. She had not turned a page even after I turned four pages.

'What?'

'It is strange, no, Roo, that we never wanted to do the usual things.'

'Define usual. In case you mean marriage and kids, that's herd mentality. I would rather be unusual.'

'Yes, we are definitely not usual. Only it is by default. I mean, if we had, you know, all normal parameters in place, we'd be wiping snot off a kid's face.'

'We'd be hunting for sons-in-law, look at our age!'
I laughed. 'Unless you are talking of grand-kids. You
know, if a daughter elopes at fifteen, comes back in nine
months with a bundle of joy, that kind of thing. We'd
make hot grandmas. GILFs, like MILFs.'

'Babies are,' her eyes were shining, 'magic. Like
holding a story in your lap, a living, growing story! And
an ending that can go any which way. A surprise ending,
a live surprise ending.'

I shrugged. How pedestrian she sounded, how
middle-class. It had never been open to me, this option
of reproducing. The least I could do was not infect
another human being with me. Like it or not, I came
with baggage, a particular genealogy. Best to bump off
this blood with me. I would be the last in line, the very
last Sen from this particular branch of the family. That
much I owed the world.

I had just about fallen asleep, thinking about his
sneakers which I had worn—all I wore, actually—the
day he took photographs of me, when she asked softly,
'And who was that guy?'

I debated whether to reply—she would presume I
had slept off—but then she would only ask again in the
morning. 'Someone who comes to my school. One of
those temp staff, on daily wages. Calls himself an artist.
I am yet to see a single painting though.'

'He looked, you know, like someone we have seen before. Don't you think so?'

'I *have* seen him before,' I reminded her.

'I think he really likes you.'

'What can I do? I am major eye-candy. Men just can't stop looking at me.'

'Seriously. You have this "I am so mature" vibe that brings us half-baked beings to you like moth to flame.'

'Because I *am* so mature. I must be older than him by… what… twenty years?'

'Thirteen,' she said and even in the dark I thought she bit her tongue.

I didn't tell her she was bang-on-target right; coincidence it might be, but I didn't want her to know that I thought it fishy, the fact that she had got the age difference right down to the year. I sighed, as if settling into sleep, and focused instead on my spectacular failure rate with men. I had a hundred percent record in dumping a minute before being dumped. Get out when the going is good, with dignity intact, hands not yet folded in beggar-bowl asana, before you bore the hell out of them, before conversation becomes only about the next meal, before they say 'I know' to what you are only thinking. It is my only superpower, anyway, to tell them the one thing they already know.

An affair is not a natural state of being, it is a mid-air

mad dangle without an oxygen mask; if you land safely, kiss the lifelines of your palms. Mixed fruit jam, I said aloud, remembering all of a sudden, but pretended I was sleep-talking when Eeedee went 'huh?'

Soon I must have really fallen asleep, waking up utterly stupefied to her shaking me by the shoulder. She was trying to shift the hand I'd used to cover my eyes and I was resisting with all my might. I came awake fighting. It took a while to clear the light of battle from my eyes and actually see her.

'Roo, it's ma.' And I remembered she too had once upon a time called her ma, who had in the first flush of her charity fit asked Eeedee to do so. Usually Eeedee got away without calling her anything.

I rubbed my eyes and sat up, my feet searching for my slippers. Found them, wore them.

We both went to ma's room. She was lying on the floor, foamy bubbles at the corner of her mouth and spots of shit marking her descent from bed, a Gretel scattering bread crumbs to find her way back home. Her tiny wrinkled mouth like the flap of rubber at the end of a tied balloon, back livid with bedsores.

'I think she is gone,' Eeedee stated the obvious. But still we had to make certain. An ambulance came, sirens full blast, took her away, declared her dead on arrival and while we waited for the death certificate to be stamped by the duty doc my shoulders started to shake. Eeedee threw me a concerned look, but then she saw I was trying not to laugh.

'What's with you?' she asked in an annoyed way.

'I told her just recently, don't worry, you are going to die.'

'You have a black tongue.'

'She had a pale heart. Didn't you hear what the nurse said?' I paused. 'Now I am an orphan, like you.'

She gave me another gauging look.

'We have no one before us, no one after us. When we die, that's it. The people who made us, the people who made them, such a waste of good fucking.'

She spoke as if from a distance. 'I had a baby.'

I had been seeing her twice a year for the last fifteen years, from the time she turned twenty-five, which was when we reconnected fully in one emotional swoop.

'You must have been very young.'

She gave me a level look. 'I was. Too young. A baby myself.'

I felt a sudden chill; had we cruelly cast her out into an unfair world, a world more unfair than we had managed to provide? 'Was it right after you left us that you got pregnant?'

'After, yes. Don't remember how much after... Those days have no date.'

'And the baby?'

'I never saw it. It was taken away before… Later I went back, but they said it had died in a couple of days. It didn't… survive.'

'All for the best,' I murmured, a little shocked by this admission. She could have told me this before, but then this is not pleasant material to share; hey, did I tell you I had a baby and it died? 'All for the best,' I kept telling her.

'I don't know… It was the timing. All wrong. Now I…' She couldn't go on. 'I wish… I wish I had a child now. I have so much love to give.'

'What are you talking about?' She was getting on my nerves. 'It is not just love. Children need parents, sane well-adjusted parents with some amount of bank balance. And they need to come in a planned manner into their parents' lives.'

She put her hand over mine. My first instinct was to shake it off. I hated condolences; they were others' way of crowing about the lack of loss in their own lives. 'I am so sorry,' they say, bending solicitously. Bullshit, you are not sorry. You are glad it hasn't happened to you. But this was Eeedee. I kept my hand right where it was, under hers.

'Roo, don't you wish too there was a child?'

I couldn't take it any more, this hee-haw. 'You have gone soft in the head. That's what this is. Or maybe ma's going has taken its toll. After all, you did call her ma. But don't let that fool you. Ma was a tough old dog.' I didn't want to say bitch, that might have not sounded too respectful to the recently departed. 'She took you in to show the world what a big heart she had. She never *mothered* you in any sense of the word. She robbed you of your childhood, at least she was an accomplice in this robbery. And what love are you talking about? This great love inside you that you go on and on about? Where did it come from? What's its origin? Because the way I see it, I got no love and I have none to give. I cannot love, and that's it.'

'Don't say that! You love me!'

'Are you crazy? Can't you see that it is just a form of atonement? For what my family did to you? I feel you suffered…'

'I still have the *Little Women* you gave me!'

Looking into her big eyes unblinkingly fixed on me, I could no longer lie to myself. I hated this girl. I had couched it well. I had even hidden it from myself. But hate her I did. She had come into the house to seize my position. Ha, I had said, I get nothing, so come share my nothing. And then papa goes and falls in love with her. Sure he went too far with this love. But he preferred her to me. To me! Words from his letters started to explode white hot in my head. Darlingest, dearliest, gudiya and nanhi nanhi nanhi. God, he'd been a basket case for her.

She was his Miranda, the little girl with big eyes papa sought to protect and cherish. Us Cordelias have no one to turn to, our love, our avowals, our declarations, our comparisons, our daughterliness never enough in the end, always, always paling before the bright burnish of our sisters' hyperbole. Lear may have come to a tragic end, but it started with him believing that Cordelia could not love.

The nurse came then with the piece of paper saying Mrs Sen was incurably dead.

Chapter 11

I ordered the cheapest funeral in the catalogue. Let her fly economy. The dead don't care for send-off parties and I had no guest list. I think I would have just left her behind in the morgue if Eeedee hadn't interfered and acted like a textbook child, murmuring softly to nursing attendants, arranging ambulance, phoning my aunt and organizing some sort of glass-topped icebox to keep ma fresh as a plastic daisy till cremation. Of course everyone, including Eeedee, attributed my brusqueness to shock. The pundit hired to mouth the mumbojumbo kept trying to include me in the proceedings. Short of saying the words 'your mother is dead' right into my mouth he did everything in his power to prod me into some display of loss. He patted my hair while leaving and looked disconcerted for the first time when I violently shook off his hand.

I lit the pyre. In fact I jumped up to light it, asking, where do I start, where?

'She is with your father at last,' said someone and I could just imagine his face if this was so.

*

Couldn't go to school for a week. Not because I didn't want to but I wasn't given a choice. The principal had come home, clutched my hand in an overwrought way, spoken in a choked voice about how she too had lost her mother, pointed emotionally to the Gulliver wreath of white flowers with our school's name prominently on it in case I had missed it, got a minion—with a rapid eye movement—to click a picture of her hugging me (for the school magazine) and lectured me on the goodness of staying indoors for seven days.

So home I stayed. And here was where Kumar found me one evening when Eeedee was out. She had said something vaguely about vegetables having to be bought. I had grunted in reply.

'I just heard about Aunty. I wasn't in town or I'd have come before.'

'It's okay,' I said. 'It was her time to go.'

'You must miss her so.'

Miss her say '*kicchu toh khao ni*' in the middle of a bowel movement? Unlikely.

He hesitated. 'Can I say I missed you?'

'You can say what you like.'

He would miss me for another day, another week max. How long can anyone miss anyone? I almost laughed. They are faithful to thee, Cynara, in *their* fashion, which is to call all they hump Cynara. (Ernest Dowson, you!)

He was silent for a while. I resisted the impulse to fill up the silence with an offer of tea.

'Your friend has left?'

'You really liked her, didn't you? That is why you are here.' My voice did not sound like I wanted it to sound. It was the opposite of cool.

He shook his head. 'I am only hoping someone is with you at such a time.'

I did not trust myself to speak again. If it was true that he preyed on older women because they made easy sexual conquests, he was hardly going to confide in me his intention to replace one middle-aged woman with another. And if I was wrong then how disgusted we all must be with me.

We sat mutely for a while, and then I got up and went inside the house. Presumably he left soon after. That whole nothing-to-say business gave the evening, gave us, a nice matte finish, I thought. Okay, so who am I addressing this to? *Stop talking to him right now! Shoo him out of your head.* Count to 10.5. Breathe in, breathe out. Visualize a flute recital. Think calm thoughts. Wish him syphilis.

The clock showed the same old time. I bid goodnight to bad days. Mornings I only see the back of, daylight's hem caught in the door. When east and west start to look the same, where art thou, O sunset?

*

At last the week was up and I could go about my life as before. There was a spring in my step, I even made some inane conversation about the weather with Eeedee, who was hellbent on packing me lunch.

I reached the staffroom and without even keeping my bag or files on the table went key in hand to open my locker. I think I knew deep down, even before I opened it, that the diary would not be there. And it wasn't. For a split second I couldn't see or hear a thing—I might as well have been suspended upside down in some timeless intergalactic highway without gravity—and then in a rush-hour montage everything I ever saw, every voice I ever heard, came at me in one go. I collapsed weakly on the floor and some tongue-clicking teachers shifted me to my chair, bending over me super-solicitously, their heaving bosoms cutting off my air supply.

I immediately complained to the principal and

even wanted to go to the police and file an FIR. What stopped me was the strange looks the other teachers gave me. One of them had the audacity to suggest I seek counselling 'as losing mothers can turn anyone nuts'! I thanked her curtly, and shut up about the diary for the moment. The general consensus was that I should thank my stars I hadn't lost any money, 'only some diary-shiary'. I tried hard, for the rest of the day, to look like I was continuously thanking my stars.

I snatched up all of papa's letters though from the locker, feeling violated on his behalf, that all his professions of love had now been read by someone other than us, him and me. They were… private. They were mine. I mean his and now mine. I stuffed them haphazardly into my bag, every last one of them, vowing to keep them super-close to me from now on. Somehow and contrary to appearances the day was at last coming to an end. My eyes were glued to the large white clock ticking on the staffroom wall, which was taking a minimum of at least three hours to go from one second to the next. It didn't help that the formerly immoral teacher kept shooting me looks of deep back-dated gratitude from time to time. Not catching her eye was a career in itself.

'You have put on weight!' A teacher who had just walked into the staffroom exclaimed loudly.

'Listen,' I told her with no change in expression. 'I don't eat or not eat with you in mind.'

'You!' she slapped my back, laughing. 'Always so funny!'

And when she went off for her class, another teacher slithered across. 'The nerve. Have you seen her backside?'

Have you seen yours, I almost asked.

*

The principal called me to her office just before the last bell. She looked very grave, like she was going to say, '*aapko* cancer *ho gaya hei*'. What she said in the same tune was: 'If you need some leave, we understand.'

I kept my eyes down, like the respectful mentally ill, wondering why her sari always ended well above her ankles. Did she know about floods before we did? Or was she going through a growth spurt? I spoilt her magnanimous gesture with a titter. Then another. I put a hand to my face to check if I was grinning. I was. What a monkey my mouth was! So I said, excuse me, for I just now remembered a joke. 'Don't ask me to repeat it,' I added quickly, panicking that she might. 'For I just now forgot it.'

I wished there *was* a joke, because she looked very much like she needed to hear one. She rang a bell on her table and in came her trusted but dim peon, whom she told briskly, 'Get the leave register.' She repeated in a louder voice, 'The. Leave. Register', as he stood there with a vacant expression, waiting for her order to percolate down his ears. Then he got it. The. Leave. Register. In the manner of man stepping on the moon for the first time, he advanced with it.

All the leave due to me was granted in one stroke. My EL and my PL and my CL and my SL, all except my ML. Earned leave, privileged leave, casual leave, sick leave, yes; maternity leave, no. But if I told her, uh-oh, I feel a baby coming on, she would have pointed her magic leave wand at me and granted me that too. She was in a godmotherish mood.

Months and weeks and days and hours stretched out ahead of me. Must buy a hammock. Or a chateau in the south of France. One of them.

I walked out of her room in a daze. She escorted me out personally, put an awkward arm around me—wait, was she gay?—and said she was sorry, so sorry. I drew back in distaste, her lisp making me feel French-kissed. 'I am not …' I said sternly, but she had already turned back, good deed done for the day.

When I got home Eeedee announced it was time she left. Left? I focused properly on her. What was she twittering on about? Go where? I had presumed with ma gone and her shop shut, she would stay with me forever and a day.

Her tone was black-tie formal. 'I have stayed here long enough, you have been most kind, but I must go back.'

Eeedee had obviously worked out that I had made those calls from her phone when I was visiting her (with the teacher's idiot husband trying to trace my calls). But why lie about it, that was the part that puzzled me. Why not just say, someone you called from my phone called back, so I gave them your number. She had been as sly as I had been. What an unsettling thought.

'Okay, go. Leave if you must. I am fine. I will always be fine,' I shouted.

She gave me the concerned look she had been perfecting ever since ma went.

'It is okay,' I said more quietly. 'I understand. We must get on with our lives.'

I didn't mention the vacation forced on me; she would think it her cue to invite me back with her, and this could go on for quite a while, me dropping her back, she dropping me back, me dropping... Oh no, I could feel a cackle coming on. I cupped my mouth, just in case. Must invest in a muzzle!

Surprisingly she made no affected speeches, no odes to indebtedness, just called for a cab and left punctually, bags in tow, in time to catch her train. I was too drained to break into opera myself.

'I have something to say,' she said at the door.

Yes, let's have it, I thought, squaring my shoulders, lining up words ASAP in my head in self-defence.

'There are potatoes in the cooker...'

Come on, just go.

We waved at each other and that was it. One hand up, one hand down, and she had made her exit. I bolted the door.

*

I got roaring drunk, sorry to say. One thing led to another and I texted Kumar. Come, I texted him. *Come*. He did not reply. This incensed me. I had presumed it was my reticence that stopped us from happening. But now I thought maybe I stepped out of his life right when he wanted me to. I went to the mirror and stared at myself. I understood his quiet. Who can want that? A frayed face, soft underbelly, a chin hair and uni-boob. My fuckable days were over.

What was that smell? The cooker! The kitchen was filled with smoke. I had to take the cooker off the hob, open windows, switch on the tiny exhaust fan, and allow the bad breath of dead food to blow over. I picked the phone. Texted, 'Creep.' Went to contacts, changed Kumar to Kreep.

Forget him, I thought, and poured myself another drink. A large safety pin that held the sides of my scalp together seemed to come apart with a click. I took the blackened potatoes out of the cooker and squashed them under my rubber chappal one by one for something to do, watching the last bits of smoke escape like smelly souls from them. Then I had to clean up the mess— the kitchen floor and my rubber chappal were covered with mashed potato, ugh—which took up some fifteen minutes. Now back at my phone, with too much time still on my hands, too much time.

I looked up, I thought I saw a shadow move. Who I used to be is still a ghost within these walls; it moves from room to room looking for me, shunting ugly lamp shades from one corner to another and the crystal frog from the top cabinet to bottom and back. Even my spectre can't sit still, then how can I? I took out my car and made my way to the address he had given me long ago, an address I never checked out. But now I weaved my way there, passing through slums called Five Star City and VIP Lane, my sunglasses making everything look like a flashback, singing as I drove some old sentimental song from a black and white film.

'Jeevan ke safar mein raahi milte hei bichad jaane ko ...'

I cried a little, then a lot. Sobbing noisily I climbed the stairs to his door. I rang the doorbell many times, no reply. I glued my ear to the door but no footstep neared the door from the other side. I began to beat at the door, like it was his chest. Eventually his landlady came out and shook a fist at me, gesturing that I come down—what emergency could there be? I began my descent with exaggerated care; the staircase seemed to be coming alive and swinging left to right, right to left. I stopped and put my fingers to my lips (like I do to quieten my class) at it from time to time; that was the only way I got it to behave, to lie still beneath my feet. I advanced gingerly and when I reached the landing below, the landlady suddenly changed tacks. 'Ma'am, you?' Her earlier angry expression gave way to one of deference.

Oh God, some ex-student. No, I was wrong. Apparently her daughter was my student.

'You seem ill,' she said, ignoring my obvious inebriation. 'Are you feeling all right?'

'Where is Kumar?' I asked, cutting through her pleasantries.

She sniffed a little at my lack of politeness, for brushing aside her enquiry about my health, and perhaps to emphasize her own lovely manners, she said, 'Dr Dhar left for his hometown today.'

I peered at her hard. She seemed real, what she said therefore must have been real. What I heard had been said. Dhar. Of course, Dhar.

He was Ela's son. The baby she spoke of. The baby that didn't die. And even in that befuddled state another thought lanced my head: was he my father's son?

I threw up then, right over the nice landlady's feet in furry pink chappals.

Chapter 12

Secrets. Things we tell ourselves never to tell anyone have a way of spilling out of us when we are not looking. Secrets bubble and boil over. In eye movements, in lip twitches. Between legs. The snitch lives in us. We give up our own secrets. We go up to people and say, 'Listen.'

Wasn't it Freud who said no mortal can keep a secret? 'If his lips are silent, he chatters with his fingertips; betrayal oozes out of him at every pore.' What Freud never said or has said but I haven't read yet or have read and forgotten is that fellow-mortals can be so taken up with, so consumed by, what they are themselves so careful to not reveal that they become blind and deaf to the quiet of others.

Secrets hide in plain sight. Eeedee had given herself away many times over each time we met, each time we spoke, but I was too busy delving into her diary, into the few words and sentences she had scribbled alone, afraid and immature, what she had put on record. The fatal flaw of all leading men—taking the extras for granted. Didn't I say so myself to Eeedee?

The fight that fateful night so long ago, calcified into some hazy-crazy hocus-pocus fast-forward movie we had watched on a faulty screen, let's zoom in on that. Post-demise rituals and police visits had pushed that night into the back of our minds. So, let's see. Papa proposed marriage to her, the first time he had done that. Something had to have prompted that. Eeedee had got her first period a year or two ago—I remember because I played middleman between her and ma for sanitary napkins, ma always granting her too few too late—and not long after, papa spoke of marriage. Why, when all was going well for him, wife and girlfriend under the same roof, good name outside, hot sex inside? And mother's insistence soon after his death, that Eeedee leave, leave now, right now, this very moment, tonight if possible. The screeching, crashing, glass-throwing decision that was taken, and some obscure relative of Eeedee's, hastily called, turning up wearily at our door, her slapdash packing, the panicked careening in and out of every room and scratching of every crevice with the cry of 'diary', 'diary', while I stood there with arms crossed, nodding at her last plea, 'It is somewhere here, my diary. Please find it and send it to me. Please.'

And whatever happened to the chain ma showed me that night? I had never seen her wear it, the black and gold beads strung together. It was a… mangalsutra, wasn't it? The price tag hanging off a bride's neck. Was it for Ela? Had ma pickpocketed it from her two-timing giddy-headed bigamy-planning husband?

The night went sleepless. Dawn broke, squeaky chalk on blackboard. Every sound grated on my ears—the newspaper falling on the front balcony, the milkman on his bicycle with large aluminium cans clanging against the wheels, children missing their school bus and leashed dogs squatting to crap. Outside a smudged pallor prevailed, like the sky had chain-smoked all night.

*

I feel the urge to say something symbolic. Like, *'Then fall, Caesar'*. But that's only a line from a dated play penned for dramatic effect.

The mirror comes up to me then. In it is a skull licked clean with dots for eyes. How frail, how human, how like everyone else I look. Retch into basin, splash water on face. Features grope back one by one—nose after mouth and thirty-two teeth. I flex my feet, feel the earth return under me, quiet as a mouse.

I call Eeedee. The number's switched off. And why not? She has everything she wants, her diary and her son. Who else but Eeedee could divine the subterranean basement buried-alive want in me to be wanted? Who else? She set that son of hers upon me like a dog, with his 'only-you, only-you' bow-bow barks. That's what she and I did deep into night whenever we bunked together, swap the castles we built in our heads. The stories we make up disclose our destinations, give away our location, where we are. I read her diary, she read what I didn't write. Oh, I had covered myself in batter ages ago, all someone had to do was deep-fry me till golden.

I tried Kumar's number. His phone rang and rang. I called from the new maid's phone. He picked up on the first ring.

'Did Eeedee tell you to sleep with me? Or was that your own bright idea?'

'Rudrakshi,' he said with false jollity. 'So nice of you to call. All fine I hope.'

'Asshole, did you hear what I said? Are you my father's son? Are you my... brother?'

Silence. I had reached him at last. I did not try his number again. I did not have to. I waited all evening and he did not disappoint me. The doorbell rang by 8 p.m. I opened the door and we looked at each other. Hungrily, the word 'starvingly' popped into my mind and I had to suppress another fit of the giggles. I was obviously dying to write a romance novel. Okay, that was what I was going to do once my mind cleared up—go on a long holiday abroad and write about beautiful people being beautiful. With nothing to worry about but what's in their pants.

Neither of us spoke. All I had in my head were half-sentences.

He looked at the carpet where I had spread out all of papa's letters and squeezed his eyes shut, a tic along his sideburn. He squatted on his haunches among them, reading without touching a single letter, his eyes jumping from one to another rapidly. 'He really loved her,' came his undertone.

'Don't we all know that!'

He tugged back his hair.

'Headache?' I asked. My temples started to throb too.

He nodded, closing his eyes.

I got him a pill; ma's insomnia one, but who doesn't need to sleep? He dry-swallowed two of them, snatching the foil out of my hand before I could stop him. Now he was going to sleep for two days in a row, the peasant.

'She always told me my father was some accountant at the college she went to.'

'What a rapeable woman your mother turned out to be.'

He flinched.

'Oh, please,' I roared, 'don't give me this sensitive shit. You are nothing but a con artist. You came here, made friends with us, with my mother and me, just so…just so you could cheat us. You engineered *everything*.'

'You lied to her. About something so important. You told her the diary couldn't be found. You have no idea what you did to her—no idea! What a nightmare her life has always been, what a nightmare it is even today. You know what all that abuse did to her, you know about her kidney transplant, right? It is mine. I lent her that kidney, that's how we reconnected. She got in touch with me when she needed… To be sexually abused at that young an age, her insides were blown to pieces.'

These nephrology tidbits she threw about, they could be genetic, maybe everyone on her side of the family succumbed to urinary infections. 'Who knows what her mom died of? Or grandmother?' I shrugged, but he wasn't listening.

'From your home she moved straight into a hospital. It was needle and thread for the longest time, they had to keep sewing her up. She was coming apart at her seams.'

'She is a liar. She got a roof over her head, little orphan Annie. And then she got a dad. My dad. Mine!'

'He raped her. No one stopped him,' he bit out through clenched teeth.

'She must have indicated he could.'

He slapped me. And I stood there holding my cheek because I knew I had gone too far. In some dim recess of my receding sanity I knew that was filth, what I just said. But having said it once I felt the need to say it again. 'Incest runs in this family. Look at us.'

He spoke like he sometimes did, in a voice older than mine, separating each syllable at birth, one slow word at a time. 'I am not related to you or your dad, okay?' He shuddered, leaving me unsure if it was a blood tie to my dad or to me that disgusted him more. 'Plus, it was consensual. Even if, hypothetically speaking, we are somehow related in some way, it would be sex between two adults who wanted to have sex with each other. My mother was raped. You were not.'

My turn to flinch now. So that's what we had been: two consenting adults. All that urgency reduced to a coy nod.

'She was a little girl in your care,' he added.

'How sexist! Foster dads, step-dads and biological dads don't molest little boys? Don't be such an illiterate.' I rubbed my eyes with the back of my hands. 'I can't believe I was taken in by you. Look at you. An upstart. Such a small-towner. What was I thinking?'

'It wasn't your mind, Roo.' His smile unfriendly, feral. 'It was your body.'

Body.

A naked electric wire word.

When he said it, as he was saying it, our eyes met, enmeshed. No, this cannot be happening. Not again and not with this sword hanging over our head. But our hands had other ideas, they reached out, they held, they stroked, they slipped and slid on each other as if we were wet bars of soap. 'You love me, you love me,' he kept chanting.

'I don't,' I snapped, though it came out like two separate sweet nothings, the 'I' and the 'don't'. 'Unless you are addressing yourself alternately in the second person and the first person. Because I can vouch for that, you love you.'

He stopped for a moment, panting ever so slightly, his eyes so close to mine we were squinting. 'We can't both be right.'

'Please,' I muttered, my need to be right more than I needed this, more than I needed him.

Efficiently, sightlessly we undressed each other and, wrist to wrist, his pulse kicking against mine, we fell into bed together like our feet had just been sliced off from under us.

He entered me snarling hot, sending all the words in my head out into the air in a whoosh. With each thrust of his the words topsy-turvied around the room and

I watched them, my mouth an open 'o', take position around the room. Till one came to a sluggish stop, stopped its clockwise and anti-clockwise spin, and stilled at long last, glowing like a top on fire. I strained my eyes: this one had come fleeing from that long-ago night, a migrant huddle of letters in no particular order. Then before my eyes they began to un-jumble, un-jam, and like reluctant dancers taking their place on stage, spelt in letters of differing font and size: S-H-A-M-E.

Shame? Whose? Mine? I shoved a rough hand into my hair and moaned. Remembering all those faceless men. Their mouths, their hands. Afterwards, when the bulb lights up not his eyes but yours, even a little toe feels naked. But that was stationary shame, parked in a basement somewhere within the body, no engine running under the hood. This shame, on the other hand, was a spectacular firework in the sky.

And it came to me crystal clear, even as my body gathered itself for indescribable pleasure on a parallel track, ma saying to no one in particular, 'Oh, the shame, the shame,' while papa, with a smug asinine grin, tightened his arm around Ela. Belonging to a generation that thought baby penises superior to baby cunts, how ma must have hated herself for not giving her husband a son, a son who would've cured all that ailed her marriage, and the possibility of a son under construction elsewhere, looming large, every night, on a bed near her, don't ask, don't begin to ask. Which was why, I realized in hindsight, she pushed me away at every step, reminding her as I did of her failure to furnish an heir. This wouldn't have happened if I had been a boy was what she must have been thinking while aiming the acid all wrong.

The 'shame' had meanwhile fallen asleep in my arms, not for him the post-coital imaginary cigarette I was smoking. When I made to move, he emitted a protesting noise from deep down his throat, and I rocked him a little. A thought struck me and I tried to shake him awake. 'What's your blood group, baby? Blood group?'

'B negative,' he mumbled, fast asleep again.

I moved away from him with supersonic speed. B negative can't be all that uncommon but it *was* my blood group. Looks like Eeedee had had her revenge, after all. I must have slept with my brother. Just like she slept with my father. The circle was complete, a circle made of naked writhing bodies, eight arms, eight legs.

From your home she moved straight into a hospital. Because she was carrying him! She had been ill with a baby. I messaged her, 'You win. What my dad did to you, your son has done unto me. Over to you.'

Immediately my phone rang. It was her. I picked it up and hissed, 'How could you stoop so low?'

'I only told him to get the diary.' She sounded hoarse. 'You are a sadist, Roo, to have kept it for so long. Why? Why would you keep it? Why would you do that to me? On top of everything else…'

'You told him to sleep with me. So that I wouldn't know it when he robbed me. Like some ingrown anaesthesia during surgery. The joke's on you. My brother's a sadist too.'

'No no no no no! Don't call him that. He couldn't… you wouldn't. You don't like men for one thing…'

'Don't be fucking naive. Anyway, you got what you wanted. You got your fucking diary.'

'You kept the diary to laugh at me, to relish my suffering.'

'That's right. That's bloody right. I wish I had made videos of your son and me.'

'No no no no no no no…'

'And *you* gave that teacher's husband my name and whereabouts, *you*! Not because they asked you about me, they couldn't have connected me to any calls,' I said, the truth occurring to me as I went along. 'You handed me to them on a platter, because you thought they were calling you about… *that* night, *our* night. And you told them I did it.'

I could picture it so clearly; her picking up the phone, anxious and alone, biting her lower lip to chapped little bits, thinking some other-worldly justice system was at work. If I close my eyes I can almost hear her childishly whisper into the phone, 'Not me. Roo. It was Roo who did it. Rudrakshi.' A name like that—not Anita, not Priya, not Sunita, not Seema, those were names other people had—convulsed the speaker's tongue and listener's ear, and pointed at me and only me. Sheer fright had made her down shutters and scoot here like a scared bunny after that.

'No no no no no no…'

This was getting tedious. I flicked the phone shut. Was she fibbing now or had she fibbed then? Was she lying that he was my father's son to get my goat, or was she yowling like this because I had got it right? I learnt one important lesson today: others can lie as well as us.

I slipped the sheet off him and lay naked alongside him—selfie time!—clicked us together and sent her the snap. This would hurt her in all the right places if he was my brother. I glanced at my lover. There is a scientific explanation for incest. For siblings and blood relatives separated at birth, it seems the pheromones go whacko at first sight. Fathers and daughters. Mothers and sons. Uncles and nieces. First cousins. Brothers and sisters. He and I. Turned on by ourselves in a way. Self-lust. But I speak for myself…

I run my fingers through his hair, he burrows deeper

into the pillow. Only the tip of his nose shows. Looks pretty much like the tip of anyone's nose. Not necessarily like mine. I resist the urge to touch my nose. I won't stop if I start.

…Because he hadn't wanted *me*, he didn't want *me*. Why do I block that out? The talk, the touch, the torch he carried, nothing was real. Not. A. Thing. He was a story he told me. A pretty story. Love, he said, love. Though I told him don't. Don't.

What if you are not the woman of his life to the man of your life?

A feeling of intense loathing roils through me. I close my eyes and it is back, that great big void from my dreams. I open my eyes, it is still here. Tired of waiting for me in sleep, it has come to claim me. I am its.

I go to the kitchen. My eye falls on the various hair oils on the sill, all in a row. Neeli bhrungadi kera thailam, dhurdhoorapathradi keram, almond oil, virgin coconut oil. So I never go bald, don't grey. For who? For him.

*

I have to do this quick. It won't do if he wakes up in the midst of it. I have to use the knife like lightning. One swipe and be done. *It is the nature of Mother Nature to bump everyone off one by one in a cosmic unsolvable whodunit.* Who said that nobody said that I said that I'm talking too much blah blah blah shut the F up. My hand, I am happy to note, does not falter. It arcs, it scythes, it stabs, like a hired mercenary hanging off my arm. And this is what I say to him all the while, shh, shh, my other hand gentle on his mouth, meeting his wide open eyes right up until the end, till they are just black lashes lying soft on his face. Shadows no more in pupils. What oh what is the South Indian for that?

I hook a finger into his belly-button and press down where the pulse is the strongest, feeling it buck, put my nose to his nose, inhale his last breath, trap it like the sound of the sea in the shell of me. Here now, not here now, we are just shadows on walls, dependent on the sun, in the end. I am sparing him the truth—all big sister, huh?

First, some music. Jackie Evancho's *Lovers.* There, much better. Anyone looking in may think it is me singing if I move my mouth a little, like this. I tear up papa's crumbling letters into small pieces, right through his nanhi and his jaan and his darlingest, so they are just so many na and ja and da, and strew them over Kumar, paper petals. The great love that got him here!

I lean closer. Is he a little pale now? No, no, rigor mortis takes a while, I still have time, I tell myself. And settle down to study him to my heart's fill; how his face fascinates me, with its deeply familiar grooves fanning off the sides of his nose, the eyelids browned genetically just so, that squarish mole, a crease in the cheek almost dimple, the pushy lock of hair on his temple… This is what I had wanted from that time he approached me in a roomful of people, as if he always knew me, as if we were meant to meet—this is all I wanted, have him to myself so I can keep looking.

It is uncanny, the resemblance. Like looking into a still pond. My outer shell, my touch-me-nots, my daredevilry, what I want no one to see, it is all right here. My mothballed baby clothes, milk teeth, a broken toy, my first cry, the hollows and black holes I was conjured up from. I moved away a bit—he did too! See, when I turn to flee, so does he. And when I come close, here he is, quick as a flash, eyelash to eyelash. I am he or he me?

'*You fly around me like a butterfly*,' Jackie is saying as I switch her off. What had he said once? Oh yeah, that we'd always been walking towards each other, with a dim memory of never having met. Here we are, baby, strangers again, let's forget we never met.

I trace his ear with my finger, lean over and lightly bite the lobe, the way he likes it (sorry, liked it; where's my grammar?) Bro, little bro. At last I can feel sisterly, half-sisterly. Is there such a thing as half a sister? Is there such a thing as half a blood tie? Can corpuscles be

Shinie Antony

snipped down the middle—this much from mother, this much from father? If so, we have identical blood flowing down one side of our veins. The other side though free to mate.

That will bring us back, as it did Julie Andrews, *to do…* the man who brought us, Kumar and me, into the world with his stray unthinking myopic, myopic sperm. Dad, dear dad, dear dead dad. *You keep disappearing, I keep getting you back. It's not the search I mind, but your inability to stay lost. The diary, your letters, your son, the sound of Roo you left behind in a mouth or two…* There he was, father mine, every time my back was turned.

Prospero and Lear at once. Magician versus madman. Peppy Prospero overtaken in the end by lunatic Lear, drowning in madness, in combat with his own mortality, laughing at gilded butterflies when himself one. Hanging on to youth by hook or by crook, wanting love from all quarters, from all daughters, and different loves from different daughters.

My turn to say to him: *We two alone will sing like birds i' th' cage.*

I loll back against Kumar. A gurgle goes up from the various open wounds, the gashes such pleased grins on him. I cup his cheek, the blood clotting in his veins, thin wine lines between his teeth, so red his colour, the colour he painted me in the fancy hotel room, the artist that he is, was. I snuggle closer, put my hand in his, and look at our joined hands, our nice inbred hands. I shall miss his eyes. Eyes that call, come out and play.

*

Eeedee should be here soon. Afraid of the dark she won't take a night bus. I can see her now, sitting tense and brittle somewhere, shoulders hunched, toes pointed, staring obsessively at the dial of her watch, waiting for morning to start her journey, to return here. Must be so tiring to forever travel, never reach. But arrive here she will. He is her only family.

A son. Accidental. Excavated only for a body part. A son who will forever remind her, with his resemblance to his roots, of how unpleasant unpleasant can get. A son grateful just to be acknowledged, to be owned. A son she exploited for herself, a non-mother come calling debts. Will she care if he is no longer there?

She is always the woman of his life to the man of her life.

So she will be back with her big bruised eyes, strung up fitful movements, and attractive speech impediment, asking for her son in halting sentences. She will get him, just not how she saw him last. She will think fleetingly of turning me in, an image of herself strong in her mind of going to the police and fluently pointing her finger at me. The words though she will have a problem with. Every word she knows has come from me. Her yes, her no. In broken, second-hand statements she will blame me for having no one, for taking away her son, the only family she had. She will point fingers, rant and rave, beat chest. And then? And then she will help me cover up what I did. For I am all she has. All.

*

I am tired. So tired. A little nap is in order now. A napette, if you please. When I wake up I will take a bath, a long bath, to wash away the blood drying on me and the sticky damp between my legs. I must have peed myself.

Wait.

A minute.

He. It is he, still in me. Warm and wet, living and breathing, talking to me, still talking, and this is what I start to hum. Hum to him. *You, you, youyouyou…* A song from my heart, not a false note in sight. He must hear this, it will make him happy. Louder so he can hear me. Louder so I don't hear me. *Youyouyou…*

What if?

That happens only in movies.

What if?

I am too old, I tell you, not fertile any more, don't you listen? Really, fuck you.

And to whom will Eeedee's house go now? The one she was leaving behind so virtuously to an 'adopted child of a friend', obviously her own son. *You live in that white villa by the beach.* He meant it was his, that I was living here, but he was the one who should have been. Our real estate scattered among strangers, like our remains will be.

What's that? Did someone just say something? The music, I check, is off. Not the gate either, too early for Eeedee to get here. I look carefully at Kumar's mouth. Nope, he's quiet. Darlingly so. The dead do tend to keep to themselves. Not me either because I am singing, remember? Shh, there it is again—caw. Did you hear that? It is the crow, someone *is* coming. That bird is never wrong.

So I am if I am. Will just have to bring him up, a son and, you know, nephew.

Acknowledgements

Literary agent Preeti Gill and editor Renuka Chatterjee for making the girl who couldn't love feel loved. Leela Joseph, G. Sampath, Preeti Shenoy, Malavika Velayanikal, Rucha Biju Chitrodia, Madhavi S. Mahadevan, Prashant Sankaran, Manjul Misra for shotgun first reads. Rashmi, Liza, Humra, Nandita, Gayatri, Krishna, Mariam, Lakshmi, Vipin, Vani, Shyni, Preethy, Lola, Sangeeta, Reena for picking up the phone. Mother, husband, daughters for picking up the... dry-cleaning?